Alethea Kontis

TALES OF ARILLAND

www.aletheakontis.com

Cover Design by Rachel Marks
Interior Design by Polgarus Studio

Books of Arilland

Enchanted
Hero
Trixter
Dearest
(Messenger)
Thieftess
Fated
Endless
Countenance
*
Tales of Arilland

Other Titles by Alethea Kontis

Beauty & Dynamite
Wild & Wishful, Dark & Dreaming
The Dark-Hunter Companion (w/Sherrilyn Kenyon)
AlphaOops: The Day Z Went First
AlphaOops: H is for Halloween
The Wonderland Alphabet
Elemental (editor)

Table of Contents

The Unicorn Hunter 1

Hero Worship 21

Sweetheart Come 29

Blood and Water 47

Well-Behaved Mermaids Rarely Make Fairy Tales 75

Blood from Stone 77

Unicorn Gold 95

Sunday 99

The Cursed Prince 139

Messenger 167

For the Brute Squad

"If you did not indulge in fantasies, how else would you know if you were living an interesting life?"

—Grumble, *Enchanted*

The Unicorn Hunter

The demon was waiting for her when the huntsman brought her into the forest. He knew exactly who she was and where she'd be and when she'd come and how she smelled and what she ate and the size of her slippers and the sound of her voice and exactly how far her chest rose and fell when she drew in a breath. From the tiniest needle on the smallest tree to the oldest dragon in the mountains, the denizens of the forest had been whispering about her for weeks now: the poor, beautiful young princess whose horrible jealous mother was sending to her death. The whole of nature waited with bated breath for her arrival, wondering at what adventures might arise from this terrible occasion. There hadn't been this much drama in the Wood since the last time his brethren had crossed the storm-tossed threshold into this accursed world.

He killed a doe while he was waiting, in part because the princess would eventually want for sustenance, but mostly because the idiot creature was too distracted by all the excitement to have the sense to stay away from him.

He knew the moment she entered the forest, for everything in it smiled at once and sighed, like a chorus of tinkling bells. The cold winter sun broke through the gray clouds and bare branches to kiss her alabaster cheek in reverence. The gold thread in her dress and golden ribbons in her ebony hair caught the light and danced like fire. She was young for her height, slender as the willows, and as yet untouched by the first blush of womanhood.

Perfect.

The four winds, dizzy and drunk with happiness at her arrival, caught up the dead leaves of the forest floor and spun them in a frenzy of dried applause. The ecstasy was short-lived, however, and the forest caught up a collective gasp when the huntsman tore the sleeve of her dress, scratched the pristine flesh of her arm, and forced her to the ground.

It wasn't supposed to happen this way. But there were demons in the world now, making the evils that men do far easier to reach. So the Memory Stone had taught the demon and his brethren, and so he knew what he must do to correct the situation.

He had hoped not to make his presence known so soon, but he needed her purity intact, and if he waited much longer all his efforts would be for naught. Her scream ripped through the now-still air. The ice pansies at his feet wept in terror. In a few long strides he crossed the clearing and kicked the huntsman with an ironclad foot, lifting his body off that of the princess and sending him sprawling in the dirt.

"I was ordered to kill the child," the huntsman said after spitting out a mouthful of teeth and blood. "What use is the rest to you, beast?"

"None of your concern," said the demon. "You have new orders now. Be gone from this place."

The huntsman came to his knees, withdrawing both a knife from his belt and a box from his cloak. "Not without claiming what's mine," he said. "I'm to return to the palace with her heart."

The demon went back to the body of the doe and sliced open her chest with one sharp claw. He plucked the tiny heart from the cavity and dropped it at the huntsman's feet. "Be glad it's not your own," said the demon.

The huntsman nodded. He snapped the heart up into the box and limped away from the demon as fast as his legs could manage.

"Oh great and honorable beast," the young princess addressed him without looking directly at him. Her voice shook and hiccuped with tears. "Thank you for saving my life. My kingdom owes you a great debt."

"The same kingdom that just sentenced you to death? I doubt they'd sing my praises at the moment." She might have been a princess and the most perfect human female form this world had ever seen, but she was still a young girl and far sillier than she looked. He'd forgotten how closely ignorance walked in the footsteps of innocence. The memory was less amusing than it was annoying. "You, however, owe me your life, and that life I will take. So stop your sniveling and get on with you. We have work to do."

"Work, my lord?"

He snorted at the address. As if her ridiculous feudal society would function longer than five minutes in his world. He felt the compulsion to explain, but knew the words would be wasted. "That's right, work. Are you at all familiar with the term?"

"I've heard of it," she said in earnest.

"Excellent. Your highness"—a ridiculous honorific as he was roughly nine feet tall, before the horns, and the top of her head came to just above his navel—"you are going to help me catch a unicorn." Actually there were three unicorns, and he intended to kill them once he caught them, but the demon felt it wise to omit these details.

"Oh, that does sound lovely," she smiled. "I accept."

Yes, indeed. Stupid as the day was long. Just as he'd suspected. He waited what seemed like ages for her to compose herself. She finally stood, adjusted the torn sleeve of her gown, collected the small silken purse she'd brought with her, and squared her shoulders. "I am ready," she announced.

"Fantastic," said the demon. "Let's go."

The demon kept a steady pace through the trees, through bushes and over streams, straight to the Heart of the Wood. The Heart was the oldest part of the forest, where the trees had forgotten more than the world would remember, where magic ran wild. There were no paths there, for only a handful of human feet had sullied those hills and valleys in the last few centuries. The Heart was where the demon had first appeared in this world. He assumed they would also find the unicorns there.

The demon looked back over his shoulder periodically to make sure the princess was still following, and slowed his pace accordingly. Every time he looked back, the forest had given the princess something else. There were flowers in her hair, she wore an ermine as a neck ruff, and the shoulder of her dress was now firmly anchored with what looked like cobwebs and a vine of some sort. She sang or hummed or whistled as they walked. She even skipped sometimes. And every time he turned back she smiled at him warily with those full, cupid's-bow, blood-red lips. He tried not to turn back very often.

He tried not to stop very often either, but her feet were small and her legs were short, and there was no help for it. Every time he stopped, the princess asked him a barrage of silly questions that had no doubt occurred to her while singing or humming or whistling and were now burning to be answered.

"Do you live in the mountains with the dragons?"

"I am from a different world, a world very unlike this one."

"How did you come here?"

How to explain using the fewest words? "The same way the unicorns did. There is a place, deep in your Wood here, where our worlds meet. The storms there are sometimes so powerful that they rip a doorway between the worlds. One creature gets pulled from my world and one from the unicorn world, and we end up here."

"How do you know all this?"

"The Memory Stone tells us so," he said. "The spirits of our demon brethren past are drawn home to the Memory Stone. It is how they share their knowledge with us."

"Do all the demons have big horns and black-red skin where you come from?"

"Most have horns. Size and skin colors vary by nature."

"Why do you wear iron boots? Are your feet like a horse's?"

"A little, yes. And I am a being of fire, so cloth or leather would do me little good."

"Why don't you wear any clothing?"

He was glad his loincloth had remained intact to avoid further such questions. "I am a being of fire. I do not feel cold the way you do. Plus, a creature who can kill anything with his bare hands has no need to be modest."

"Why didn't you just kill me?"

Not that it hadn't crossed his mind. "Because I need a living innocent to lure a unicorn. I've had little success with dead ones."

"Have you seen a unicorn?"

"Once, briefly." One had arrived at the same time he had. Such was the balance.

"What are unicorns like?"

"Like giant white puppies of happiness."

"Do you think the unicorns will like me?"

"They will think you are the best thing they have ever seen." Like everyone else, it seems.

"Do you like me?"

"Only when you're quiet."

"Why are we capturing a unicorn?"

"Because it's the only way I know to get home." Again, he thought it wise to omit the rest.

"Do you have a family back home? Do you miss them?"

"I do need you alive, but you don't need your tongue." This answer was enough to curb her examination until the next time they stopped. It wasn't a planned rest, but the girl collapsed on the crumbling stones at the foot of an ancient well. It was as good a place as any. A bear cub snuggled up to the princess's back and a warren of rabbits cozied up to her front, keeping her warm. The demon thought it a bit ridiculous that nature here should fawn all over a little girl just because she was beautiful and a princess. He felt bad for any poor ugly pauper girl who stumbled into the forest unawares. She'd be that bear cub's breakfast for sure.

Every time they stopped there was always one animal or another in the princess's lap. The demon noted their bravery. In all his time in the forest, he had never before had the pleasure of any beast's company; they sensed what he was and stayed far away. The more intelligent creatures still did, but it seemed some of their children were young enough to tempt fate.

Turning the tables, he asked her one question before her heavy eyes escorted her into sleep. "Why aren't you afraid of me?"

"Should I be?" she asked.

"I'm a demon," he said. "I could drink your blood to warm my feet and grind your bones to make my bread."

"But you won't," she said. "You need me to capture a unicorn."

"I could burn all your clothes so that you might freeze. I could spit in your face and you would lose your beauty in a heartbeat."

"Will you?" she asked.

"Perhaps, if you make me mad," he said.

"Then I will endeavor not to anger you." She yawned. "We have tales, old stories from long ago of benevolent beasts who were really kind souls, or princes in disguise."

"I am no prince," he said.

"Pity," she mumbled. "I could use a prince." And with that, she slept.

Perhaps the queen was not mad, and in sending her daughter away she had done her kingdom a favor. This child, though a rare beauty, was too happy and silly and gullible and kind. Her subjects would riot and her advisors would rob the coffers bare and her castle walls would be breached within a fortnight. She would make a terrible queen.

Even still, he could not imagine sending his own daughter, or any child, to her death. And he was a demon.

He leaned back against the stones of the well, safer from his body heat than a tree, and closed his own eyes in relief. This world was so cold—not to his skin, but to his heart—and it wasn't just the winter season having washed all the colors with the stark dullness of mud and snow. What little fire existed in this world was buried far underground, so far that being away from it tore at his mind, trying to free the madness there that would be all too happy to escape. His brethren had succumbed to that madness. Eventually, so would he. Even now he could taste the princess's pulse beneath her skin, imagine his claws marring her perfect flesh, smell the fear of the wild animals who dared accompany her. He wanted to destroy the forest around him, dead limb from dead limb, and set it ablaze so that there might be color and warmth filling this world, if only briefly.

If he did not destroy the unicorns soon, their presence would tip the balance too far. It would cause another storm and rip another of his brethren from his world. He needed to kill those unicorns now, all of them, the first two for his brethren and the last one so that he could escape this prison and end the dreaded cycle...for as long as Chaos would let it be ended.

He woke and realized he'd fallen asleep. The stones beneath him had melted away into the dead earth. On the far side of the well the princess sat, quietly singing and gently combing the hair of the latest beast in her lap with a jeweled comb. Of course the princess had taken a jeweled comb into the woods. Then again, she hadn't expected to survive this long.

The animal in her lap seemed to be an albino fawn or a large goat, and then the demon realized that what looked like an ice shelf behind them was actually an icicle protruding from the animal's forehead. The first unicorn. The demon would have laughed if he hadn't been afraid of scaring the beast away. There the princess sat, shimmering like magic, her skin darker than the unicorn's by a mere blush, the curtain of her ebony hair like a waterfall of shadow between them. From her blood red lips came a nonsense song about flying dishes and talking pigs. A rainbow of feathers fluttered in the trees around her; a congregation of birds had flocked just to hear her sing, and the unicorn was mesmerized. Its eyes were closed and it suffered the princess's combing without complaint, completely still.

Too still.

The demon crossed over to the princess in a few steps that shook the ground and caused the myriad inhabitants in the bushes to explode into the air. The unicorn did not move. The demon reached down with a large hand, the skin of it as red as her lips, the claws as dark as her hair. She stopped singing when that hand came into view, and she stopped combing, but the unicorn's head in her lap held her trapped.

The demon swept back the unicorn's silken white mane with a claw; a few stray hairs stung his skin. The perfect flesh beneath the mane was crisscrossed with layers and layers of angry red lines.

The princess looked confused. The demon gently took the jeweled comb from her hand. Its aura of bile taunted him. "Poison," he said. He melted the trinket into slag with the heat of his palm and tossed the little golden ball of it into the well where it could do no more harm. "Did your mother give that to you?"

The princess nodded silently. One big, fat, shimmering icedrop of a tear slid down her cheek and fell onto the unicorn. Into the unicorn. Another tear fell, and another, deeper into the unicorn's flesh as it turned to snow in the princess's arms. When she realized what was happening she jerked, startled, and the shape of the unicorn crumbled to cold lumps of nothing in her lap. She lifted her arms slowly, reverently, and the rising sun made the rime on her forearms sparkle. Dazed, she raised a shining finger to the tongue that waited between her blood red lips. The demon slapped her hand away. He pulled her up by the wrists and began dusting and melting every bit of corpse-ice on her that he could see.

"Stupid girl," he muttered.

"What would have happened," she asked when she found her voice, "if I had tasted the unicorn?"

"You would have screamed with delight because it would have been the most delicious thing you've ever put in your mouth. But after unicorn, all other food to cross your lips would taste foul. You would wander the world for the rest of your life, starving, forever trying to taste something, anything, that comes close to that divine perfection."

"Oh," she said, and clasped her traitorous fingers behind her back. "Thank you," she added, but sounded unsure.

"Come," said the demon. "We should leave this place. Other unicorns will sense that one of their brethren has died here and they will not come near it."

"I'm sorry," was all she said.

"Why?"

"I did not let you capture the unicorn. I killed it."

"No matter," said the demon. "There are others. Let's go."

The princess was navigating the melted stones of the well in her thin, inadequate slippers, when something occurred to her. She brightened and reached for her tiny clutch, pulled a small object from it and held it tightly in her hands. She squeezed her eyes shut and scrunched up her face, as if in pain. The demon held his breath, waiting for a magic spell or another bout of weeping to burst from her. Though possibly more trouble, he hoped for the former.

"I wish my handsome prince, my one true love, would find me and save me and take me away from all this," she said, and she tossed the coin in the air.

The demon stretched out a hand and easily caught the tiny gold disc before it hit the well. His palm, still hot from the comb, melted it, too, into slag. He tossed the thin, swirling, misshapen bit of metal into the snow at her feet.

"Why did you do that?" the princess asked.

"You didn't want to make that wish," the demon replied.

"I didn't?"

"You don't want any prince who would have you right now," he said. "Trust me."

"But I always make that wish," she said.

"Then I hope he takes his sweet old time finding you," he said.

"Wishes are magic and wonderful," said the princess.

"Are they now?" said the demon. "'Skin as white as snow, hair as black as ebony, lips as red as blood...' How'd that wish work out for you?"

Those blood red lips formed a thin red line, and the princess stomped away from the well. The demon chose to enjoy the silence.

They marched through the forest as before, with a varying menagerie of wild animals keeping pace. The princess was distraught when the demon picked one new friend at random to be their lunch, but once cooked her growling stomach betrayed her and she ate with relish. She apologized to her friends when she finished; they seemed to accept it easier than she had. And so she frolicked with them as the day and miles through the endless forest stretched on. The meadows gave way to hills and then mountains, and at times they had to skirt sheer cliff sides and rocky terrain, but still they walked. The princess had long since shredded and discarded her delicate slippers, her ebony hair was as stringy as the limp ribbons still woven through it, and her golden dress trailed behind her in muddy rags, but she maintained her posture and addressed her wild friends with all the pomp and circumstance of royal courtiers.

They did not stop again until they came to a stream that sliced a deep crevasse through the forest and rushed swift with icemelt water from the mountains. The princess was far ahead of him, singing a harmony with a family of larks and dancing with a fluttering collection of moths and butterflies, so she did not spot the unicorn refreshing himself in the stream until she was almost upon it. The demon noticed at once; he had felt the chill presence of the unicorn emanating from the water, far stronger than icemelt.

The princess stopped her dancing, though the circus around her did not, so she still appeared to be a flurry of movement. She lifted her mud-heavy skirts and curtseyed low to the unicorn across from her, on the opposite bank of the narrowest part of the stream. The unicorn noticed her, lifted his head from the water, and bent a foreleg as it bowed to her in return. Without taking her eyes from the animal, she reached into the silk purse at her belt and withdrew the most beautiful red apple the demon had ever seen.

It occurred to the demon to wonder why the princess had not mentioned the apple during her passionate fit at lunchtime. It did not occur to him to wonder why she was possessed of such a remarkable fruit in a season where similar apples had long rotted into memory. And so he did not stop her when she offered the apple to the unicorn with both hands, and it munched heartily. For a moment they were a mirror of snow white skin and blood red lips, a picture of innocence and perfection.

When the unicorn started to scream, it sounded very much like how the princess had screamed when she'd been attacked by the huntsman. Its cry cut through the oncoming twilight and pierced the heart of any living thing within earshot. Some of the smaller animals in the glen did not survive the terror of that scream. The demon thought it wise not to mention this to the princess.

She was already crying, screaming in fear as the unicorn screamed in pain. She leapt into the icy stream and threw her thin young arms around its slender neck, mindless of its spastic hooves and rolling eyes and blood-frothed mouth. She ceased her cries and began to sing to the beast, a lullaby, in an attempt to calm it.

There was magic in her voice, whether she had willed it there or not. The demon saw several animals curl up in sleep as they heard the song. He yawned twice himself. The unicorn's thrashing slowed with its heartbeat, and it laid its head in her lap, far less gracefully than the previous unicorn. She rocked it back and forth, back and forth, all the time singing it to sleep. Singing it to death. She held the unicorn until long after it had turned to snow at her feet and the wind had blown its form into tiny drifts around her.

The demon approached her gently this time. He did not want to disturb her, but he also did not want her to freeze to death, so he loosened his fire essence through his iron-shod feet and into the ground, warming the earth around her. The corpse-ice of the unicorn began to melt away.

"I am sorry," she told him again when the tears were gone. "I killed the unicorn."

"No matter," he replied calmly. "Can I get you anything?" He found himself surprised at his concern for her welfare.

She untied the silk purse at her waist and held it out to him. "A drink of water from the stream, please," she said. "There is a golden cup in my bag." Her voice was ragged and hoarse with strain and sadness.

The demon snorted. "You humans and your gold." He was careful with his giant claws so that he only untied the small bag instead of ripping it to shreds. He withdrew the ridiculously ornate cup; like the comb, it, too, burned at his eyes with its sick aura. "Your mother gave you this." It was not a question.

"Yes," the princess affirmed. "She gave me the bag to take with me on my journey."

He cursed himself for his own stupidity and immediately immolated the bag and all its contents at his feet.

"No!" cried the princess, the unicorn now all but forgotten.

"Why would you want any of that?" he asked. "Every bit of it was meant to kill you."

"It's all I have," she said over the blackened mark of singed earth. "It's all I had to remember her by."

"You have your memories," he told her. "Those should be painful enough."

She stood tall and glared at him, her whole body rigid, her hands in tiny fists at her side. "How many more unicorns are there?"

"One," he answered.

"How many more demons are there?" she asked.

"One," he answered again.

"What happened to the others?"

"I killed them."

She relaxed a little in sympathy. "How could you do that?"

He could just as easily ask her how she could have killed two unicorns, but he thought it wise not to mention it. "We are not meant to be here in your world. Not us; not the unicorns. Our presence makes the spectrum of your world larger. We make the waves taller, the valleys lower. We turn bad into evil and good into divinity. The longer we are here, the more we lose control of our minds. Demons become savage. Unicorns, I imagine, become more ephemeral. Our souls belong in our own worlds, and they return to these worlds after our death."

"So you hunted down your brethren and killed them for the sake of my world."

"And to save their souls. They were easy for me to find; evil begets evil. I would not have found the unicorns without your help."

"And how would you have killed them?"

"I don't know," he answered honestly. "You did that for me."

The princess exhaled then, deflated, and sat again. She hugged her knees to her chest and looked out over the rushing, icy stream. Apart from the burbling of the water the woods around them were blessedly silent. The demon sat beside her, only close enough to warm the ground beneath her and the air around her.

"Is that why my mother is so evil?" asked the princess. "Because there are demons in the world?"

"Perhaps. I don't know."

"I don't think you are evil."

"Then you are a silly girl."

"Are unicorns demons too?"

This was certainly an avenue of thought the demon hadn't considered. "What makes you say that?"

"They have horns, and hooves, and they are elemental, and they are the polar opposite of you. They are ice where you are fire. You said that demons are all different colors based on their nature. Are there ice demons where you come from?"

"I have not heard tales of any."

"Perhaps they were exiled from your world. Or you from theirs. Or perhaps we were the ones exiled. We might have all been part of the same world once."

"That would be a remarkable history," he said.

"What will happen to you when you die?"

"My soul will be returned to my world and I will tell my tale to the Memory Stone, so that others who might follow this path will know how to act."

"I don't want you to die."

"I have to. My continued presence here will only tear your world apart."

"I know," she said matter-of-factly. "I just wanted you to know."

"Thank you," said the demon. Her declaration both pleased and frustrated him. She was growing too mature too fast. He hoped it didn't affect her ability to attract the unicorns.

"Shall we go find this last unicorn then?"

The demon stood, offering one large, clawed hand to help the princess to her feet. She took it. "We shall."

Just beyond the stream was another small mountain, more of a large hill, with a gaping maw before them that appeared to be the entrance to a mine. "Up or down?" the demon asked her. He imagined the unicorn would find them either way.

"I want to see the stars," was all she said before she started climbing.

They climbed to the summit in the long hours of the early evening. In the spring, the demon suspected this ground was covered in wildflowers. What crunched beneath their feet now was only dirt and dry grasses hiding sharp rocks. The princess stumbled a few times, but she kept on climbing. The demon could not see the blood on her feet, but he could smell it on the wind, and so long as she said nothing, he wondered why he cared.

Once atop the small mountain, the princess skipped and jumped about joyously under the bright heavens. She ran around the summit as if the wildflowers still surrounded her. She spun and spun and threw her head back and held her hands up to the sky to catch the flakes of snow that had started to fall like little stars all around her. And then the stars themselves began to fall from the sky and dance with her. The princess pulled the golden ribbons from her hair and tied them all together in one long strand, and the stars leapt and swirled and twirled the ribbon as she spun it around herself. Her giggles and laughter sounded like bells. The wind around her whooshed and whistled and sounded like whinnying.

And when the whirlwind of flurries took a unicorn's form, she quickly tied her ribbon around its neck, fashioning it into a crude golden harness. The great white beast bowed his head to her, accepting his defeat, and allowed her to lead him to the demon. With one quick hand, the demon snapped the horn from the unicorn's head; with the other, he slit its throat, deep and deadly. Without so much as a snort the unicorn burst into a flash blizzard of snow, covering both the demon and the princess in blood and ice.

The demon lifted the unicorn's frozen horn to his lips, and the heat from his breath melted it quickly down his throat. His stomach clenched and his muscles spasmed; the poison was quick.

There were tears in the princess's eyes. The demon held a large, warm hand to her small, cold cheek. "I'm sorry," he said. "I killed the unicorn."

"I cry not for a beast I never knew. I weep for the beast who was my friend."

"Where will you go?" he asked, no longer surprised at his concern for her welfare.

"I will find whoever mines this mountain and seek shelter with them." She was above him now; he did not remember lying down. Her ebony hair curtained her face, erasing the stars from the night. From her neck dangled the melted coin she had almost thrown in the well; she had woven one of her golden ribbons through a hole in the design. He reached out to touch the medallion, but his arm did not obey.

"Perhaps your prince will come," said the demon.

"In time," she said. "Perhaps in a very long time, when we are worthy of each other."

"Very wise," said the demon.

"Will you tell your Memory Stone about me?" she asked.

"Yes," he whispered. "I will tell it all about the smart and brave princess I once knew."

She laughed and fought back the tears that no longer fell. "There is no need to lie."

He laughed too, but his breath had left him. "And what stories will you tell your world?"

"I have"—she screwed up her beautiful face in an effort to maintain her composure—"I have my memories," she said. "Those should be painful enough."

He nodded in reply, but his head would not obey. He fought to keep his eyes on her face, but he suddenly went from looking up at her to looking down upon them both. He watched her as she hugged herself to his chest, then shifted herself around his horns so that she might cradle his head in her lap. She held him until he turned to ash in her arms, until all that was left of him were his iron shoes. He watched her until his corpse-dust flew away on the wind, until his soul was drawn so far away that she was only a golden speck on the dark mountainside, another star in the sky.

He had been wrong. She would make a great queen.

Hero Worship

To: Mister Jack Woodcutter
From: Miss Sonya Vasili

Dear Mister Woodcutter,

My grandmother bade me pen this letter. She says that when someone saves your life, especially a legend such as yourself, the least you can do is write them a proper thank you note. We also mention you in our prayers to the gods every night. Sorry if that sounds a little creepy, but if it weren't for you, Baba Vasili and I wouldn't have anymore prayers—or anymore nights, for that matter.

"Thank You" doesn't seem a big enough phrase to fit all the meaning I need it to, but as I haven't been able to think of another, more appropriate gesture in the last few weeks, Baba Vasili handed me the quill and parchment, and here I am. Please forgive as well my utter lack of eloquence, as this is a tradition to which I am not yet accustomed.

And lest this silly little note (if it even finds you on your Grand Wanderings) finish without saying: THANK YOU. Thank you, Mister Jack Woodcutter, again and again. Thank you for my life.

All the best,

Sonya "Red" Vasili

To: Jack Woodcutter

From: S. Vasili

Jack,

I hope this letter finds you as successfully as my previous pitiful note, but even if it doesn't, that's all right. The writing of it alone is enough. I can close my eyes and imagine you're right there in the settee listening to me, the only person in the world who believes me. Yes, Baba Vasili was there, but she is tired of listening. She doesn't want to hear about the nightmares (I see the wolf's teeth, I feel the brush of his fur, I smell his breath, and I scream for you). She is tired of me jumping at shadows in the forest. The other girls at school have started calling me "Little Red," as if I am just another silly baby telling tales.

Baba Vasili will not tell the tale because she does not believe in spreading evil out into the universe, so no one believes me. No one will listen. No one will stand beside me. I am alone. I have no one. No one but you. And I don't even have you, as you gallivant off on your adventures. But I will write to you often and share my pain. I know you won't mind. It eases my heart a little.

I wonder if you dream of the wolf, if he haunts your head with his darkness as he haunts mine.

I wonder if you dream of me.

Sonya (Red)

Jack—

I miss you. Does that sound stupid? We met during one of the worst moments of my entire life, but I miss you. You shone like the sun, did you know that? Such a bright light against the darkness of the wolf. Against my darkness.

But of course you know. Everyone knows of your beauty, your confidence, your ability to bear impossible burdens, perform impossible tasks, and beat unbeatable foes. The bards sing your praises from mountain to ocean side. I'm sure you never sleep in a cold bed.

You must think of me sometimes, the in-between moments before sleeping and waking. Do you see me, my wide eyes, my long auburn hair, my pale arms desperately reaching for you as I did in that moment? So very innocent and frightened and powerless in your strong embrace.

Most days, I sit on this hillside and pluck the petals of daisy after daisy. (You love me every time.) I see your eyes in the cloudless sky and your hair in the sunshine. Your chest is the tree trunk supporting me as I lean back against it. I inhale and the breeze is your breath, and in those moments we are together and I know—

I *know*, with all my heart and mind and soul—that you can feel me too.

I miss you, Jack. I miss you.

And I love you.

—Red

My Dearest Jack,

A troubadour came through town last night, singing for his supper. Once his belly was full of Baba Vasili's rabbit stew, he indulged me with hours upon hours of The Adventures of the Illustrious Jack Woodcutter. I never tire of hearing the trials and triumphs of my one true love, however great or small, for I know that one day those songs will hearken your return to my pale young arms and pining heart.

But as the evening drew to a close (and the singer was so far into his cups that I was forced to tie him to the chair), he related to me a silly, bawdy shanty about The Great and Powerful Jack running afoul of a basket of poisoned pastries.

I cannot apologize enough, for I know those pastries could only have been mine. (Did you recognize the basket from that fateful night so long ago? I shed blood, sweat and tears over that basket then; I thought it only fitting to do so again, for you.) I can only think that the messenger crossed paths with a vengeful fairy, or that some of the ingredients spoiled in this unnatural autumn heat we've been having. You know that I certainly never meant to harm you in any way!

However, in the event that you had taken a turn for the worse, I would have sensed it immediately and been fast by your side to nurse you back to health. You never need call, my Jack, for my heart knows you. I believe in your absence that I am developing the ability to sense when you are in danger. (Obviously, had the pastries been a real threat, I would have known about them long before that soused balladeer.)

The gods brought us together, Jack. We are a matched set, cut from the same cloth. Who am I to deny the gods? I only hope they see you safely home soon, my dearest. I will be waiting. As always.

Ever Your Girl,

~Red

Beloved,

This will be my last missive to you. The pain cuts me deeply, and soon I will return to the nightmare mouth of the wolf, where I was always meant to be. There is no world without you. There is no me without you. And soon, there will be no world at all.

Forgive the stains on the page, red as my hair, but the quill grows heavy in my hand, heavy as my stone heart. The beats are slower now. The breaths are faint.

My soul is crying out to yours, growing ever blacker with the night. Hear it and come to me soon, my love. Look to the stars—they will guide you to me. Perhaps you are already here, with your ax at the door. I only hope it is not too late.

—R—

To: Mister Jack Woodcutter
From: Anastazia Yaga Vasili

My dear Mister Woodcutter,

Sir, it pains me to bring such news to you, after the incredible good deed you did my granddaughter and me so long ago, but in the event that any—or all—of Sonya's letters have found you on your travels, I thought you would want to know.

Red is safe. It was I who dragged her back from the jaws of death this time, but the eyes and ears and hands of the enemy were her own. Its teeth were the penknife I keep in the writing desk.

It was I who encouraged my granddaughter's correspondence to you, so it is only fitting that I must bear the burden of its outcome. You and I only saved Sonya's body from the wolf that night—the part we could see and touch and feel. Her mind, I fear, never recovered from that darkness, and I did not recognize the signs until it was almost too late.

Our little Red is recovering in the care of my spinster sister, high in the remote reaches of the white mountains. Perhaps you might have heard of it in your wanderings. Cinderella's blind and mutilated stepsisters convalesce there. So, too, do the young girl with the donkey's tail on her forehead, and the one who spits snakes and toads when she speaks. I believe Red is in the best hands possible. If my sister cannot save her from the wolf, no one can.

As much as I hate to burden you with this information, I thought it best that you should know. You are a great man, sir, and you once did my family a kindness that will never be forgotten. May your road be straight and your skies be blue. May the gods lift you to their breasts and find you worthy enough to be rid of your burdens. Many blessings to you.

Your servant,

Baba Vasili

To: Miss Sonya Vasili
c/o Baba Yaga's Traveling Home for Unfortunate Young Women with Magical Maladies

Dear Red,

Get well soon.

~Jack

Sweetheart Come

asha was fourteen when the villagers threw her to the wolves.

She was mute: a quirk that eventually unnerved enough people to justify her banishment to the Wild Wood. She surprised them all by emerging from the Wood many months later without a scratch and heavy with child. This time it was the villagers who were struck speechless, but—enchanted or cursed—no one challenged Sasha's right to be there. Upon her daughter's birth, Sasha caught the midwife with her haunting gray eyes and said, "Mara," clear as a bell. The rest of her secrets she kept. By the next full moon, Sasha was gone.

Mara was raised by the midwife, embraced by the villagers, and ended up earning her keep as a huntress. Her tracking skills were unmatched and she had a sixth sense about her prey—virtues which kept the food stores well-stocked through the cold winters. When

Fate found the man to tame her wild nature, Mara had one daughter, Rose. Rose "had a nose," and grew to become one of the most sought-after cooks in five counties. The man who sought out her heart instead of her pies was a humble woodcutter, and together they had a daughter named Aurelia, with a voice that could sing the sun down from the sky. When she was of age, Aurelia took up with a band of wandering minstrels, and so was the first since her great-grandmother to leave the village. She and her beloved fiddle player were also the first to bear a son, Bane.

Bane had a shy smile, a quick wit, and a heart of gold. From his grandfather, Bane learned how to cleave a piece of wood in two with one stroke. From his grandmother (and from experience), he learned to tell the difference between good mushrooms and bad. From his father he learned to play a variety of instruments well enough to coax out a melody for every occasion, but he preferred the fiddle. From his mother, Bane learned how to sing the sun down from the sky. Every evening they would trek to the edge of the village, to the top of the hill that looked down over the Wild Wood, and they would farewell the day. The selections varied with their moods and the seasons, but the last song was always the same lullaby Aurelia had sung to her son every night since his birth.

Have wonderful dreams, love
And dream while you wonder
Of things that are sure as
The sound of the thunder
Love leaves too sudden
And death comes too soon

And wolves they all bay at

The full of the moon

When the sound of his fiddle surpassed that of his voice, Bane played instead while his mother sang. And when his grandmother's apprentice herb-girl returned his shy smile, he asked her to marry him. And when Harvest became pregnant with their child, the nightmares began. For the first three months, one came at every full moon. Bane dreamt of running through the autumn trees at twilight to the top of the hill, hair brushed with dew by the welcome chill of the wind. There, along with his brethren, he turned up his face and howled to the sky. Harvest teased him about his twitching and the soft whimpering noises he made in his sleep.

In the second three months, the dreams increased with both frequency and intensity. Bane imagined himself grooming, hunting, mating, and feeding kits. He awoke angry, amorous, and exhausted in turns—sometimes all three at once. In the daylight hours he found himself resisting the urge to rub his face in the cool spring grass or growl at the rabbit vermin that ran amok in the garden.

In the seventh month of Harvest's pregnancy, Bane's dream-self fought brutally with a wolf from another pack. He awoke on all fours, looming over Harvest and staring at the crescent-shaped marks on her pale white throat. She had slapped him out of his vision; his cheeks stung from the deep scratches her prenatal nails had raked across him. In the midnight silence, a drop of blood fell from his face to her breast.

"Sweetheart," Harvest said calmly, "this has to stop. You have to go to the wolves and ask them for help."

On any other day those words might not have made a lick of sense to him, but right there, bathed in bright moonlight, with the salty taste of his wife's sweat and fear fresh upon his tongue, Bane knew what he had to do. When dawn broke, he packed up his fiddle and a blanket and set out for the hill at the edge of the Wild Wood. Harvest stayed behind at the garden gate, but not before handing him a small bag of food. She had noticed the look in his eye, the look of every man who has left home with no idea of when he might return, or if he should.

"Sweetheart, come back to me," she said as she embraced him. "Come back to me before our baby is born."

Bane kissed his wife hard, with all the love in his golden heart, and promised that he would.

Bane went to the top of the hill that overlooked the Wild Wood and stayed there for three days. He fiddled from twilight into the wee hours of the morning. He played until his throat went hoarse and his fingers bled. He collapsed on the cold, hard ground as the sun rose, breathed in the lingering scent of his wife on the blanket, and slept the day away. He woke in the late afternoon, broke his bread and had a small meal, and waited. He lifted his fiddle and bow in time to farewell the sun, and continued to serenade the waning moon until he could continue no longer. The wolves did not come.

The next day, Bane walked down the hill and into the Wild

Wood. He walked through spider webs and sunlit meadows. Every morning he slept, every evening he walked, and every night he lifted his fiddle and bow and sang into the twilight. He slept fitfully on beds of hay and early summer wildflowers that made his golden heart ache for his wife and unborn child. Impatient and frustrated he wandered and played, played and wandered, deeper and deeper into the Wild Wood. Still, the wolves did not come.

After the new moon, after the darkest night in the thickest part of the deep Wood, the dreams returned. Some days he would wake without clothing, his skin covered in angry red scratches. Some days he awoke with blood caked on his lips that was not his own and a full belly. Sometimes he awoke so far from where he fell asleep that he spent the rest of the day following the scent of his blanket back to his fiddle. The smell of his wife was fading; Bane feared that one day he would awake and not be able to find his way back to it. To her.

Still every night he played, the calluses on his fingers growing thick as his limbs grew thin. He played songs of long ago and songs of yesterday. He played songs of adventure and songs of loss. He played teaching songs and drinking songs, songs of life and songs of death, songs for family and enemies. When he had played them all he made up new songs, songs for Harvest and their unborn child, and as he sang he wept tears onto the wood of his fiddle. But he always sang the sun down and up with a variation of that same old tune his mother had taught him.

I dream as I wander

And wandering dream

Through a wild and dark Wood where
I'm not what I seem
I'm lost and I'm lonely
And so with this tune
I call to the wolves
By the light of the moon

At last, on the first night of the full moon, Bane's song was answered by howling. He thought it was his imagination at first—he had imagined many things in his dream-wracked wanderings: the sound of Harvest calling his name, the smell of her skin, the warmth of her breath on the back of his neck. Invigorated, Bane ran up the nearest hill, climbed atop the largest rock there, and started the song again. Beneath his rough beard his smile grew with every howl and his golden heart ached to be so very near the end of his torment, to be so close again to the peaceful life he had before it was rudely interrupted by dreams of a life he didn't want.

The wolves poured down through the trees, their sleek bodies undulating in a neat, dangerous wave. They bound up the hill with predatory speed and encircled the rock on which he stood. Each wolf moved with preternatural grace in a dance as old as the hills themselves, ears perked up, mottled hair bristling, sharp teeth flashing, and for the first time it occurred to Bane to be afraid. He simply poured that fear into his song and used it to fuel his playing as the wolves settled in around him.

In the glow of the moonlight he could hear their breath, taste their scent, smell their fur, feel their hearts beating as one. In the glow of the moonlight his golden heart warred against itself—the half that yearned for freedom and his place in this pack, and the half that yearned for home and the rest of his soul. The circle of wolves parted and, in the glow of the moonlight, the alpha pair stepped forward and became human.

The male grew tall and lean. A thin coating of dark gray hair still covered his body, little enough for Bane to tell that every muscle was tensed and ready to strike if any of his suspicions were confirmed. The female was similarly wiry yet petite. The fuzz that coated her breasts and belly was mottled gray and russet; the rest of the hair that had covered her lupine form now cascaded down her back. There was something not quite right about her face, as if the human mouth she now wore couldn't accommodate all of her tearing, bone crunching teeth. But she pinned him with a yellow stare, and when she spoke, her words were clear.

"Come," she said, "come run with us, cousin."

His blood roared through his veins, pumped wildly through a heart as golden as her eyes in a mad rush of acquiescence. But her invitation had sounded too much like another plea his mind replayed every night when he collapsed in exhaustion and every morning when the sun nudged him awake: *Sweetheart, come back to me. Come back to me before the baby is born.*

"I cannot," he said, and there was far more regret in his voice than he intended. "Please," he implored. "Make the dreams stop."

She stretched out a hand to caress his bare foot, where it dangled down from the rock on which he sat. Her mate growled low in his throat. Her long, narrow palm was warm and rough, the nails that tipped her fingers dark and thick. It would be nothing for her to thrust those nails into his chest, tear out his traitorous golden heart, and replace it with moss and tree sap. "These dreams you dismiss so easily," she said, "they are my dreams."

"I am sorry," he said, and again the words dripped with regret.

"It is not a decision to make lightly," she said. "If I take the dreams from you, any part of you that was ever wolf will be gone forever." No more seeing in the dark. No more singing to the moon. No more smelling his way home. But he could not return to his wife and family-to-be as he was, so dangerous to their well-being and so much less than a man.

"Come run with us, cousin," she asked again. "Be sure that the choice you make is the right one."

He set his fiddle on the rock, hopped down into the swarm of giant, hungry wolves, and slipped his hand into that strange and deadly palm.

Harvest didn't tell her parents about her husband's mad journey for fear they would come and take her away. Her home was the one thing that kept her tethered to sanity. Bane's family was very supportive: During the days, Rose helped her in the garden and her husband built a crib for the nursery. In the evenings, Aurelia and the fiddler played and sang for their supper, lullabying their daughter-in-law and soon-to-be grandchild into bed. For all the well-meaning company, it was the dead of night Harvest lived for most. She would stare out the window, wish on the stars, and blow kisses to the bone-colored moon. She would listen for the creaks and whispers that echoed in the empty corners of the dark world. They had the timber of Bane's voice and they promised her they would return home before their baby was born. They promised.

The night there was no moon Harvest felt the loneliest she'd ever been in her life. But were it not for the absence of her celestial companion, she never would have noticed the yellow eyes watching her from the far side of the garden. At the same moment there was a kick in her belly—she gasped, and in a flash the wolf was gone.

Harvest looked for the wolf every night, and every night it was there. It never approached the house, simply watched the house from the same spot at the opposite edge of the garden. Harvest felt an irrational kinship with the wolf. She imagined that they were both lonely, both burdened by responsibility, both waiting for something they weren't exactly sure of, and both wanting something they knew they only had a slim chance of obtaining. But the hope was there.

Harvest began leaving food out for the wolf, sometimes not finishing her evening meal on purpose so that there would be scraps left. She walked them as far as she dared, to the near edge of the garden. She never saw the wolf's eyes in the daylight and she never saw it eat, but come dawn the bowl was always empty.

The first night of the full moon, Harvest walked the bowl of scraps out to the garden and saw an old man standing where her wolf had been. Short, dark gray hair covered his skin evenly, barring shocks of pure white on his forehead and temples. He was darkness, but for his sharp teeth and those piercing yellow eyes.

Harvest dropped the bowl and squeaked out a tiny shriek, immediately wishing she was a braver woman.

"I liked you better as a wolf," she said.

The wolf-man laughed hoarsely at her statement, baring his mouthful of deadly teeth in the process. Harvest froze, ordering herself to remain calm and show no fear. This was one of the last times her baby would be able to feel her every emotion, and she refused to let cowardice be one of them. *See, baby, your mother is strong. One day, you will grow up and be this strong.*

"You must come with me," said the wolf-man.

"I do not have the dreams," said Harvest. "That is my husband."

"It is for your husband's sake that you must come," said the wolf-man. "I fear for the loss of your husband to the wolves."

Harvest found his phrasing odd—it sounded more like the wolves would steal him away rather than kill him. "He will come back to me," Harvest said defiantly.

"The wolves can be rather persuasive," he said.

"He will come back to me," Harvest repeated. "He promised."

"Yes," said the wolf-man. "But what if he is not capable of keeping that promise? What if he needs your help?"

"Then I would come with you," said Harvest without hesitation. She pulled her kerchief from the pocket of her apron, tied her hair back, and walked across the garden to the wolf-man's side. With a nod and a blur that sparked through the hair on her arms, he quietly transformed back into a wolf and bound into the darkness, leading Harvest step by trotting step to the heart of the Wild Wood.

She followed him to the top of the hill that overlooked the

Wood, recalling the many evenings she had sat with Bane and Aurelia or softly sang along while they serenaded the sunset. Harvest had a small voice, like a chickadee, but her notes still rang true. Aurelia had the voice of a whippoorwill, throaty and loud, with seemingly endless stamina. Bane's voice was a dove's, low and haunting. When he sang of love it made her yearn, and when he sang of loss it made her cry. Harvest placed a hand on the cool, smooth bark of the tree where she had sat to watch him, an invisible silhouette against the moon, and she felt both those things. The wolf huffed to get her attention and she followed him down the hill, into the Wood.

The pair of them made good time, for all that she was so heavily pregnant and he was so terribly impatient. The wolf would growl every time she had to stop to rest, but she knew him for the old man he was and could tell it was all bluster. He growled as well when she paused to look for herbs: greens to keep her strong and flowers to keep her nourished and roots to keep the baby from kicking his way out of the womb before she was ready. Before her beloved sweetheart fulfilled his promise.

They walked in fits and starts until dusk of the next day, or when the trees grew so thick it was hard to tell when day ended and night began. Harvest found a mossy patch on the north side of a large tree that seemed the least rocky and bug-infested. She sat with her back to the tree and crossed her arms over her belly. She wished she had thought to bring a blanket, or a slice of bread, or a chunk of cheese, or her sanity. She wished she had something of Bane's with her, something that might draw him like a lodestone.

Something that might speak to him if he could no longer understand her words. The baby flipped over inside her, settling down for the night and reminding her that she did have something of Bane's. The most important thing of all.

She shivered again and the wolf approached her, slinking out of the shadows with his head and tail down to show that he was not a threat. Not knowing the proper way of things, Harvest risked stroking the wolf's muzzle with a gentle hand. The shock of white stared up at her like a third eye seeking deep into her soul. His charcoal fur was thick and rough and smelled of pine and grass and dirt and musk and blood and strength and ferocity. *You have some of that strength in you, baby. One day you will grow up to be this strong.* She sighed. *And one day, I hope your beloved is not chasing you into the Wild Wood.*

The wolf knelt down and laid that giant, dark head full of teeth in her lap. Harvest stroked his fur absentmindedly and let his warmth seep down through her legs and up through her belly into her neck and shoulders and arms. Still worried, yet safe from harm, Harvest let herself sleep.

It took Harvest and the wolf less than five days to reach Bane's rock, as they were tracking prey and not lost or wandering or falling asleep and waking up somewhere else every other evening. And all the strength and all the stamina Harvest had been absorbing from the moon and the wolf and the Wood suddenly left her. She stretched her arms up until she felt her shoulders pop, pulled her husband's fiddle down from the rock, and collapsed. The tears she shed over the mahogany fell in the same places as the tears he had shed over her, before he had transformed into a beast that did not keep promises because he no longer knew what promises were.

Grief and fear and sadness overtook Harvest, seizing her body in violent spasms, and the babe—rightfully so—decided he wanted no part of it. Harvest screamed into the empty daylight. The wolf snapped at the air in frustration. The ground beneath her, already damp with her tears, now muddied with the babe's rushing preamble. "Come back to me," she whispered to no one. "Sweetheart, come back to me."

The old wolf was gone even before she finished speaking, leaving Harvest alone with only the wind and the air and what courage she was able to summon between bouts of racking pain. Her baby was tearing her body apart, her husband had shattered her heart, and she had clearly lost her mind. She wondered how much of her soul had to be torn away before even the gods didn't recognize her anymore. She wondered about the color of the sky, and exactly how much grass she could pull up with one handful. She thought about her own mother, and Bane's. She thought about the tune they played to sing down the sun, the tune that called the wolves. The fiddle reminded her of the melody, but she couldn't remember the words through the pain, so she made up her own.

I'm missing my sweetheart
My sweet heart does miss
The sound of his voice and
The feel of his kiss
The wind it blows colder
The day's light grows dim

But damned if I'm having

This babe without him!

Harvest laughed loud, giddy, hysterical, frantic, and on the next wave that lifted her back off the ground, she saw the wolf pack surrounding her. There was too much love and too much hate and too much of every other emotion warring inside Harvest for her to pick one. As there was only a half moon peeking through the twilight clouds, the female who spoke to her changed only her face so that her words might be understood. She sat neatly, with her long tail wrapped around her paws like a canine sphinx with a mouthful of knives.

For a moment, the pain was so sharp Harvest could not feel her legs. She broke a sweat maintaining a level voice. "Let him go."

"Our cousin runs with us by choice," said the face.

Harvest bit the inside of her lip until she tasted blood. She refused to lose her courage in the face of her adversary. As the pain tore through her in deeper, more frequent bursts, she repeated the only words left to her.

"Come back to me," she asked the sky, for she knew not which wolf in the pack was her husband and that pain dwarfed the babe's like a tear in a rainstorm. The charcoal wolf—her wolf—nudged one beast forward and she saw that its eyes were blue-green, not yet the bile amber-yellow of the rest of the pack.

"Come back to me," she said to him. Her husband recognized her with those still-human eyes—eyes that had traveled just as hard a road as she—but she could tell he did not understand her words.

"Come back to me," she whispered once more. It didn't matter that he had left her. It didn't matter that he now wore a skin of fur and walked on four legs. It didn't matter that she had been forced to walk leagues to track him down. He was here and the babe wasn't born yet; there was still time to keep his promise.

"If he returns to you," said the sphinx, "he will forsake every part of his wolf blood." The bitch had the nerve to preen after her statement. Had she been within arm's reach, Harvest was sure she could have snapped her neck.

Harvest lay back on the rough ground. Invisible thorns pushed their way into the ends of every nerve in her body. She took deep breaths and saw pinpricks of light. Beyond them, a few bright stars sprinkled across the heavens like the rocks under her spine, stars she had wished on since she was old enough to know what wishing was for. "Go then," she said to those stars. "For he has now forsaken me."

A wolf approached her, but it was the charcoal gray. The elder brushed her neck with his muzzle, then leapt over her seizing body to follow the tails of the pack that had already left him behind.

Harvest broke her nails in the dirt and concentrated on the wind and the air and the babe tearing its way out of her. *Courage, little one*, she told it. *It's just you and me, now*. Wind and air and pain. Breathe. Wind and air and pain. Breathe. Wind and air... and a hand on her forehead. She opened her eyes to see Bane standing over her, scrawny and shaggy and smelly. His blessedly furless skin was riddled with angry scratches and bruises as deep and purple as the skin beneath each of his blue-green eyes, and it was the most beautiful sight Harvest had ever seen.

The remnants of his wolf magic fled from his palm into her body, Harvest could taste and feel and smell and live it as it waned, healing her heart and filling her womb before it died completely. As her burdens lifted, the babe escaped her body in a rush of fluids. Bane wrapped his son in the blanket he had left behind and the three of them lay quietly together under the stars.

In addition to a certain amount of strength, stamina, and the ability to see in the dark, Bane lost his voice. He still spoke a little, but his words growled out from low in the back of his throat. There would be no more singing for him. He could still play, though, and when the rest of his memories came back to him, he accompanied his mother to the top of the hill in the evenings to sing down the sun. Harvest made the journey as well, carrying baby Hunter until he was old enough to walk. She sang as well, and though her voice never carried the force of Aurelia's, it grew from that of a chickadee into a lark.

It was spring before any of the wolves dared show their faces. When one did, it was that of the charcoal gray elder. He came to them at the full moon, and it seemed that his coat was sprinkled with far more white than Harvest had noticed previously. She was glad he had returned, so she could properly thank him for fetching her and protecting her. Bane was less happy about the wolf's presence.

"Why are you here?" he snapped. For all that he was pure human now, he acted more like a wolf than before.

“I have come to ask your forgiveness,” said the elder. “Our female trapped you, and in doing so, she put you in danger.” He looked down at the babe Harvest cradled in her arms. “She put all three of you in danger.”

“I want nothing from you,” Bane growled.

“The gift is already given,” said the elder. “Whether or not you use it is up to you.”

“What is it?” asked Harvest.

“The gift is the song,” said the wolf. “We took much from you that made you valuable, and for that we must give something in return. Balance must be maintained.” He motioned down to the fiddle that hung at Bane’s side. “Play the song you know,” said the elder, “the song with which you farewell the day. The song with which you called the wolves. If you play the song as you walk through the Wood, no harm will come to you.”

“There is no song,” said Bane. “I can no longer sing.”

“The magic is in the melody,” the wolf said to him. And then to Harvest, “The words are yours alone.” He placed a palm on Bane’s chest. It startled him out of his scowl, but he did not flinch away. “You may not have yellow eyes, cousin, but you still have a golden heart. Perhaps one day you will find forgiveness there.” He let his hand fall. “Not today. But one day.” He turned to leave, but Harvest stopped him.

“What of our son?” she asked. “Will he experience the same thing when his first child is born?”

“It will not take him as strongly and it may not come at the same time,” said the elder, “but he will have to make a choice one day, as all young men do." Harvest mirrored her husband's scowl and the wolf laughed. "Worry not, little mother. Your son has your strength. He will survive. We all will."

Bane and Harvest watched the wolf walk across the garden and into the trees until the shadows swallowed him. Bane lifted his fiddle to play the song once more and Harvest added the words—her own simple words in her clear, simple voice.

And just as it should, son
Our happy tale ends with
Our family three and
A wolf for a friend
If life makes you lonely
And trouble's your boon
Just sing this wolf song
By the light of the moon

Bane drew out the last note almost longer than the night itself. When Harvest turned to look at him he stared back at her, his golden heart smiling through his blue-green eyes. She cradled their babe in one arm, and the other hand she held out to him. "Sweetheart, come in to dinner."

Bane lowered his fiddle, slipped his hand into her soft, delicate palm, and followed behind them.

Blood and Water

Love.

Love is the reason for many a wonderful and horrible thing.

Love was the reason I lived, there in the Deep, in the warm embrace of the ocean where Mother Earth's loins spread and gave birth to the world. Her soul was my soul.

Love is the reason she came to me in the darkness, that brave sea maiden. I remember the taste of her bravery, the euphoric sweetness of her fear. It came to me on wisps of current past the scattered glows of the predators.

The other predators.

Her chest contracted and I felt the sound waves cross the water, heard them with an organ so long unused I had thought it dead.

Help me, she said. I love him.

The white stalks of the bloodworms curled about her tail. We had a common purpose, the worms and I. We were both barnacles seeking the same fix, clinging desperately to the soul of the world. Their crimson tips brushed her stomach, her breasts. They could feel it in her, feel her soul in the blood that coursed through her veins. I felt it too. I yearned for it. A quiet memory waved in the tide.

Patience.

My answer was slow, deliberate. How much do you love him, little anemone?

More than life itself, she answered.

She had said the words.

I had not asked her to bring the memories, the pain. There is no time in the Deep, only darkness. I could but guess at how much had passed since those words had been uttered this far down. Until that moment, I had never been sure if the magic would come to me. Those words were the catalyst, the spark that lit the flame.

Flame. Another ancient memory.

The empty vessel that was my body emptied even further. I held my hands out to her breast, and there was light.

I resisted the urge to shut my inner eyelids to it and reveled in the light's painful beauty. It shone beneath her flawless skin like a small sun, bringing me colors...perceptions I had never dared hope to experience again. Slivers of illumination escaped through her gills and glittered down the abalone-lustered scales of her fins. Her hair blossomed in a golden cloud around her perfect face. And her eyes...her eyes were the blue of a sky I had not seen for a very, very long time.

She tilted her head back in surrender and the ball of light floated out of her and into my fingers, thin, white and red-tipped, much as the worms themselves. I cupped her brilliant soul in my palms and felt its power gush through me. So long. So long I had waited for this escape. I had stopped wondering what answer I would give if I should ever hear the words again, ever summon the magic. When the vessel was full, when my dead heart beat again, would I remember? Would I feel remorse? Would I have the strength of will to save her, to turn her away?

You will see him, I told her.

She smiled at me over the pure flame of her soul.

I was a coward.

I pressed her soul into my breast. The moment the light filled me I became her. I could see my body through her eyes—translucent white skin marred by jagged gills, blood red hair tossed up by the smoky vents and tangling about the worms, black eyes wide, lips parted in ecstasy.

I could see him in the back of her mind, the object of her affection. He was tall and angular, with sealskin hair. There had been a storm and a wreck, and she had saved him. She had dragged him onto a beach and fallen in love with him as she waited for him to open his eyes. She had run her fingers through his hair, touched his face, traced the lines of the crest upon his clothes. He was handsome and different and beautiful. When he awoke, he took her hand in his and smiled with all his heart. And when he kissed her, she knew she would never be able to live a life without him in it.

In that small moment, as the glow of her soul dimmed into me, she told herself it was worth it.

Once the transformation began, the pain pushed all other thoughts out of her head. Water left her as suddenly as her soul had left her, her gills closing up after it. The pressure that filled her chest made her eyes want to pop out. She clamped her mouth shut, instinct telling her that she could no longer breathe her native water. She beat furiously with her tail, fleeing for the surface.

Halfway there, the other pain began. It started at the ends of her fin and spread upwards, like bathing in an oyster garden. The sharpness bit into her, skinning her, slicing her to her very core. Paralyzed, she let her momentum and the pressure in her chest pull her closer to the sky. Part of her hoped she could trust the magic enough to get her there. Part of her didn't care. It wanted to die, and knew it could not.

That price had already been paid.

Her head burst above the waves and she opened her mouth, letting the rest of the water inside her escape. Her first full breath of the insubstantial air was like a lungful of jellyfish. She coughed, her upper half now as much in agony as her lower half, not wanting to take that next breath and knowing that she had to.

She lay there on the undulating bed that was once her home and let it heal her. She stared up at the sky until it didn't hurt so much to breathe, until her eyes adjusted, until rough hands plucked her out of the sea.

She was dragged across the deck of a ship much like the one from which she had rescued her lover, right before it had been crushed between the rocks and the sea. The man who had pulled her up clasped her tightly to him. He was covered in hair, more hair than she had ever seen in her life, and in the strangest places. It did not reach the top of his head, but spread down his face and neck and onto his chest. Perhaps it liked this upper world as little as she did and sought a safer, darker haven beneath his clothes. She reached out a hand to touch it, and he spoke to her. The sounds were too high, too light, too short, too loud. She did not understand them. His breath smelled of sardines. She ran a finger through the hair on his face, and he dropped her.

Misery shot through her and she collapsed on the deck. Her hair spilled around her...and her legs. She stared at her new skin. It looked so calm and innocent, but every nerve screamed beneath it. Another man stood before her now, wearing more clothes than the hairy man and shiny things on his ears and around his neck. His bellow was deeper than the first man's but still as coarse and profane, and still foreign to her. He crouched down before her and brushed her hair back from her face. He cooed at her. She touched the bright thing around his neck that twinkled the sun at her, and he grinned. His teeth were flat. She wasn't threatened. Braver now, she pulled at the necklace. He let her slide it over his head and put it around her own neck.

He picked her up and carried her to a place that hid her from the sky and set her somewhere softer than the deck. She liked this place and this man who now worshipped her. He had given her a gift, and now he would take care of her. If only there was a way she could tell him why she was there. She was sure he would help her. Perhaps he could see into her heart and just know.

The man removed his shirt, and she relaxed even more. He wanted to put her at ease. By looking like her, he would make her feel like she belonged. He took off the rest of his clothes and came up beside her. He patted her head, ran his hands down her hair. He touched her breasts, her belly and her legs. Still sensitive, she brushed his hand away. He put it back. She tried to push it away again, but he was stronger. She frowned. He smiled all those flat teeth at her once more. She wondered if she might have been mistaken. He moaned, parted her knees and entered her.

The misery she had felt before was nothing compared to this anguish. She inhaled the excruciating air and screamed a hoarse cry. She clawed at him, pushed at his weight on top of her, but she could not move him. Agony ripped her body apart again. A tingling sensation washed over her and the light in her eyes began to dim. Somewhere in that darkness, through the pain, she could feel his heartbeat. The emptiness in her cried out. He had something she needed.

She reached up, pulled him to her, and sunk her pointed teeth deep into the skin of his neck. She drank him down, consuming his soul, filling the barren places inside her. He collapsed on top of her and still she drank, until there was nothing left.

The door burst open and the hairy man entered. He pulled the naked man off of her. He could tell what the man had done from the blood between her legs. He could tell what she had done from the blood she now licked from her lips.

"Siren," he whispered.

She gasped. In her brain there was an avalanche.

Words flooded her, images and thoughts, smells and sounds. Knowledge. She cried out again and slapped her palms to her head. She had taken the man's soul, and his life right along with it. She watched as the shafts of her golden hair turned deep red, filled with the captain's blood.

The first mate had named her. He knew what she was. She was death, the shark, the thing to be afraid of. She lured men to their graves with her beauty.

In one swift motion he pulled the knife from his belt. She did not flinch as he approached her. There was nothing left to fear.

The knife swept down and split the captain's throat open, hiding the teethmarks in the cut. He stared deep into her eyes as he pulled a large ruby ring off the dead man's finger and put it on his own. The knife, streaked with what little crimson was left in the captain's body, he brandished at the crowd of men gathered at the door.

"Eddie Lawless, what's goin' on?" the man in front asked. The men behind him whispered low, words like "magic" and "evil" and "witch" catching in her ears.

"It's Lawson, Cooky," the hairy man responded. "Cap'n Lawson. An' don't ye forget it."

"Yessir," the men mumbled. "Yessir, Cap'n."

"Leave me," Lawson ordered.

"But sir, what about Cap'n—"

"*I* am the cap'n," he told them. "Ye can collect the carcass later. Leave me now." He slammed the door in their faces.

The mattress shifted under his weight as he sat down across

from her. She did not want to look at him, concentrating instead on the ends of her new hair and the line across the dead man's throat.

Lawson shoved the body onto the floor. "Siren."

She looked up.

"So. Ye can understand me then."

She nodded once.

"Good." He pulled the sheet down and wiped his knife blade with it. "Understand this. I know what ye are, what ye need and what ye do. If ye do exactly as I tell ye, I won't kill ye."

If she had known how to laugh, she would have. It was unsettling. She knew what laughter was, what caused it and why someone did it, but she didn't have the slightest idea of how to make her body perform such a feat. It was the same with the words – she could understand them, but she couldn't get her tongue around them and speak back. She would have laughed at the thought of this man killing her, for she would have welcomed death. But there was one task she meant to accomplish before that happened. She had to find her lover.

She nodded her head once more.

"Excellent." He left the bed and went to open a trunk on the other side of the room. He rummaged through it for a moment, and then tossed a bundle of burgundy material into her lap. She stared at it, marveling in the slight difference between it and the color of her hair. She reached out and stroked its softness, drawing patterns on it with her finger.

His chuckle brought her out of her state. "Ye 'ave no idea what to do with it, do ye?" He took her by the hand and gently eased her off the bed. "Come on, stand up."

She placed one foot flat on the floor, then the other. Then she pushed up with all her might, locking her knees and propelling herself forward into him.

He caught her before she hit the floor. "Whoa. Easy. Ye 'ave to get yer sea legs." He helped her balance enough to stay upright. Surprisingly her feet held her without too much trouble.

"Now," he said, grabbing the bundle off the bed, "ye're lucky I 'ave a daughter an' I'm used to doin' this." He spun her around so that she faced the wall. "Six years ago I only knew 'ow to *un*dress a woman." He pulled her hands up above her head and eased the material down around her. He moved her hair to one side so he could button up the back.

"There." He turned her back around. "It's a bit large an' it'll probably be a tad warm. But it'll keep the sun off ye, and the...my...men away from temptation." He looked her up and down. "Not that they'll need much warnin', mind. But ye get enough rum into a man...well...stranger things 'ave 'appened."

He looked down at the former captain's body. "Ye won't need to...eat...again for a while then?"

She shook her head.

"Right. Best if ye only do it when I tell ye." He shoved the knife back into his belt.

Her eyes widened.

"Oh, don't worry," he chuckled. "Ye're aboard a pirate ship, darlin'. If there's one thing we've always got more than our share of, it's blood."

He wasn't wrong.

They encountered a ship three days later. There were blasts from cannons spread amidst the cries of men. She lost her footing when the ship lurched sideways, hooks pulling the losing ship close enough so that men might cross over. She peeked through the windows at the smoke of the guns, swords clashing as the blood flew.

Lawson came back to her room when the battle had died down. He opened the door and threw a man down at her feet. His clothes were ripped and his face was a bloody mess. Gray eyes looked up at her from the red-stained face and filled with terror.

"No…oh, God, no" were the last words he spoke.

His fear was intoxicating.

She closed her eyes when she was finished and let the magic wash over her. It wasn't just the blood she craved; it was everything. She needed the senses and the feelings, the emotions and the pain, the good and the bad. She needed his life, his soul.

Rejuvenated, she tossed her hair back and peered up at Lawson. He cupped her cheek and wiped a spot of blood away from the corner of her mouth. "There's my girl." He threw open the door and kicked the man's body over the threshold. "There's yer cap'n, men," he bellowed. "Seems 'e got into a spot of trouble. Any of ye want the same trouble, just cross me."

Crews were mixed and booty was swapped, and then they were off in search of the next victim.

The second ship they burned. It was spectacular. She ran to the railing and held her hand out to the beautiful, live thing that danced on the sea as it consumed sails and timbers and bodies alike. She had seen candles and lamps, but this was a beast, wild and hot and bright as the sun. Hands grabbed at her clothes to keep her from falling over the rail, and they pinned her down when the magazine finally exploded, taking the rest of that ship's crew with it.

On the third one, she found him.

The battle this time was a long one, and by the time Lawson brought her the captain of the other ship, he was half dead. She drank him anyway. And somewhere in the memories of this man was the someone she had been looking for.

She gasped when his face came to her. She drew back, her teeth disengaging from her meal, blood running down her chin and staining her dress. This man knew her lover. Not well, but he knew him. She tried to make sense of the jumble of images that flowed through her, but nothing connected. She searched his body for a sign, a hint, something. She found it on the smallest ring he wore, a gold band stamped with the crest she had traced over and over on the beach that day.

When Lawson returned, she pointed at herself and then held up the ring. He smiled and patted her on the head. "O'course ye can keep it, darlin'. Ye can 'ave all the trinkets yer little 'eart desires."

He didn't understand. How would she make him understand? She slid the ring over her red-tipped thumb. She would save it until she thought of a way.

The fourth ship was a long time coming.

She spent most of that time at the bow of the ship. The crew didn't grumble much about having a woman on deck. Most of them apparently didn't consider her a woman. Lawson made it plain that he enjoyed having her there. Word was getting around about Bloody Captain Lawson and the Siren. They struck fear in the hearts of men and made quite a profit as a result, so if anyone had disagreements, no one made mention of them.

Lawson called her their figurehead. It was an apt description, based on what she had seen on the prows of other ships. She would lean against the rail, arms spread, red hair trailing behind her in the breeze. She liked letting the wind slip through her fingers. It reminded her of home. The currents of air were not that different from the currents of water. Men did not have the freedom of movement that her kind enjoyed, but the principles were the same. They walked among it, breathed it in, let it give them life. It brought sounds and smells to them. They did not see it or think to taste it, but it was always there in them, touching them, surrounding them.

She stood there, day after day, until the salt encrusted her lips and her hair was a burnished orange. What little red appeared in the tips of her fingers had been burned there by the sun. The men avoided her and prayed hard for another ship. They tread lightly around the captain. No one wanted to be the Siren's next meal.

Lawson finally bade her return to the stateroom, and she was too weak to disobey. The table was covered in maps and charts. She walked past them on the way to the bed and glanced down at the area Lawson was plotting. A symbol caught her eye, and she jumped back. She waved at Lawson. She pointed to herself, and to the ring around her thumb. She pointed to herself, and to the same symbol down on the map.

"There?" he asked her. "Ye want to go there? Why?"

She could not answer, so she just kept pointing to herself and the map.

"That's 'ome," Lawson told her. "Where Molly is. I promised never to go back until I 'ad a ship full o'riches. She deserves no less." He shook his head. "No, darlin', we can't go there. Not yet."

Frustrated, she closed her eyes. Disjointed thought flashes skipped through her mind. She tried to remember the man with the ring, tried to bring his soul to the surface. But it had been so long, and she was so weary…and there was a port…

Her eyes snapped open. She moved her finger on the map to an island just off the coast of the country bearing her lover's symbol. She pointed at Lawson, and then stamped her finger back down on the map.

"There? What's there?"

She threw her hands up in exasperation and scanned the room. She held up the medallion of her necklace to him.

"Gold?"

She nodded and kept searching. She found his knife on the table, picked it up, and then shook her head.

"Swords?"

She shook her head again.

"This?" He removed the pistol from his belt and held it out to her. She nodded emphatically.

He cocked his head and grinned. "Siren, if ye're right about this,

I'll take ye anywhere in the world." He strode out of the room and hollered to his first mate. "Hard to port, matey!"

"Cap'n?" the first mate asked.

Lawson hooked his thumbs in his belt. "We're goin' 'ome."

The greatest tale of Bloody Lawson and the Siren is the Massacre at Windy Port. Legend has it that their ship, cloaked in dark magic, slipped by the watchmen unnoticed. Once docked the crew cut a gruesome swath through the town, led by Lawson and his Sea Witch. Lawson brandished a rapier in one hand, a pistol in the other. The Siren, dressed in fine burgundy velvet, marched through town before him, seducing men to their grisly deaths. Her eyes were as black and cold as a shark's, her hair a mass of ebony fire waving about her. They left none living in their wake, took what they wanted and stole back into the night as invisibly as they had arrived.

Like most legends, not a word of it was true.

They sailed into Windy Port under a royal flag they had appropriated from a previous hunt. They docked without incident, the crew scattering to the winds to pick up intelligence, hefty bar tabs, and the occasional whore.

The moment Lawson set her down on the dock, she fell. The hollowness inside her throbbed. She could not believe anything could have been so still as land. There was no life in it. The air was not strong enough to keep it fluid. It was rock. Still, empty, dead rock. She was but a shell, a humble reconstruction of the world upon which man walked every single day. How did they survive without a connection? She hugged her stomach, doubled up and gagged, only emptiness escaping her dry heaves.

"You okay, honey? Take it easy. It'll pass soon."

The words spoken to her had a cadence she had never heard before, and it surprised her so much she didn't understand them at first. The hands that pulled her hair back away from her face were small and delicate. The woman had on a black dress. Her hair was pinned up on her head and decorated with shiny black beads. She smelled...soft and nice. And she was gentle when she accepted the Siren's embrace.

"It's all right," the woman said as she patted her back. "Everything's going to be all right."

She didn't scream when pointed teeth pierced her flesh.

Everything was going to be just fine.

Suddenly conscious of her appearance, she pulled her dress over her head and began tearing at the woman's clothes. Lawson knelt beside her and motioned for his men to surround them so as not to draw attention to the scene. "Discovered vanity, 'ave we?" he chuckled as he helped her undress the woman's corpse. Once she had changed, the men weighted the body and rolled it into the ocean.

Lawson helped her stand. He tossed a dark cloak about her and covered her hair with its hood. She was glad he didn't force her to wear shoes—it was hard enough enduring this much separation from the water. She didn't know how much more she would be able to bear.

The inn they went to almost pushed her sanity over the edge from sensory overload. The room was filled with people of all shapes and sizes. There were smells from the food, the ale, the dogs in front of the fire, the fire itself. Men and women talked and shouted and joked and laughed. A scrawny youth crawled up beside the dogs at one point and sang for his supper. She was mesmerized. These were so different from the songs of the water, the flash of fish in the currents, the mating of whales in the deep. Some were slow and soft; some were fast and loud. And when the rest of the room joined in, she clapped her hands in merriment.

The crew dropped in one by one to report and consult with Lawson throughout the night. There were nods and low whispers. She watched as papers were signed and money changed hands. Thus Bloody Lawson conquered Windy Port, without ever leaving his seat. When the festivities ended he paid for his meal, tipped heavily and left, dragging his cloaked companion behind him. It was the sailors and merchants that returned to their vessels the next morning and found them empty or missing who took their anger out on the citizens of the port. Lawson and his crew were miles away before the massacre even began. Bloody Lawson and the Siren were never heard from again.

Several months later, Edward Malcolm opened a waterfront inn in the capitol city named The Sea Lass. He purchased the house next door as well. It had a master suite and a nursery and a very large kitchen that could be used to supplement the inn's in case of overflow. One of the rooms in the house had a door with seven locks. They were installed the day before Molly's return from school.

Molly's homecoming was a grand event. Lawson, now called

Edward, had covered every flat surface in the house with sweets and cakes and flowers. He had hired a seamstress to take Molly's measurements for a whole new wardrobe, the only one that didn't seem overly preoccupied with the Prince's upcoming wedding. Paper-wrapped packages of all sized littered the largest of the tables. A doll and a rose waited on the chair for his princess.

The Siren sat on a stool in the corner, cut off from the sun and the earth, the water and wind. She waned as she watched the miniature cherub-faced human run through the door to embrace her father. Her mop of dark brown curls disappeared in her father's coat as she hugged him, right before he picked her up and twirled her around the room. There was something about this strange apparition, this child, and she could not decide what it was.

Molly giggled as she snuggled her doll. She reached out to the rose.

"Be careful," her father warned her.

"Yes, Papa," she said smartly. "I will watch for the pricklies and the thornies." She buried her nose in the crimson petals and took a deep breath. When she opened her eyes, Molly saw the Siren there in the shadows.

The child set her doll down carefully on the table. "Who is she, Papa?" Molly whispered.

"She's…" he started, twisting the ruby ring on his finger. "I saved 'er," he said finally.

"She's so pretty," Molly said. The child came around the table and held the flower out to her. "She's just like the flower."

"Yes," he said. "Just like the rose. She's got pricklies and thornies too, Molly. You have to be careful around her."

Molly took another step forward, still offering the flower. The Siren took it and grinned, being careful not to show any teeth. Before her father could stop her, Molly launched herself into the Siren's arms.

The child's skin was softer than the woman's at the pier. Her hair smelled of sugar and...something...indescribable. She took another deep breath. There was life within this little bundle, so much life she all but vibrated with it.

Edward wrenched her away. He took her by the arms and held her tightly. He sank down to his knees, so that he could address Molly eye to eye.

"Don't ye *ever* go near 'er again," he said sternly.

"But Papa, she's so sad," Molly cried.

"She is dangerous," he admonished. "Just be a good girl and do as yer papa says."

Molly bowed her head. "Yes, Papa."

"We'll even call 'er Rose, okay? So ye don't forget." Edward chucked her under the chin. "Now, what are ye gonna name yer dolly?"

Molly's eyes brightened again and she rushed back to the table for her doll.

The Siren sunk her nose into the flower and inhaled sugar and sweetness while she watched the child open the rest of her gifts.

That night as he escorted her to her room, he said to her, "Ye touch my daughter, I'll kill ye." Then he shut the door and turned seven keys in seven locks.

Each day after that was much the same. She was not allowed to leave the house, and the third time Edward caught her staring out the windows, he forbade her that too. Each night he would take her to her room and give her the same warning about his daughter before turning the seven keys of her prison.

She would sit on her bed and stare into the darkness, wondering what she had done wrong. Had she not given him the riches he desired? Had she not paved the way for him to return home to be with his daughter? She had made him happy—why should she suffer as a result?

She edged closer to the window and watched the moon move across the sky. Somewhere not far, the reflection of that same light was skipping across the waves. Somehow, she would escape from this prison. Someday, seven locks would not hold her.

Every few nights he would bring her someone, long after Molly was asleep. He would wake before the dawn and take the body away. She learned all she could from these poor souls, but it was never enough. They were whores or cheats or liars, people whose absence in some way benefited Edward and whose minds were such a jumble of unreliable information she could never discern anything that could help her.

She waited. She waited while he scolded her every night. She waited as he shoved each of the seven bolts home. She waited as he fed her, sparingly, enough to survive. She waited for him to get comfortable, to slip, to let something get by him.

Like the snitch.

Edward bent over and the unconscious man fell from over his

shoulder and onto the bed before her. “Small, but ‘e’s all ye’ll get, understand?”

She opened her mouth, throat contracting. “Yeth,” she managed to say.

“Good. ‘Cause if ye touch my daughter, I’ll kill ye.” He shut the door. She counted slowly to seven before pulling the man into her lap and feasting.

Her heart pounded with a foreign pulse.

He was there.

Her lover.

He was everywhere inside this man’s head. He sat at the head of a table, talking sternly to a group of older men dressed in black. He sat in a large chair at the end of a hallway. He rode a horse down the path through the garden and along the beach. He rode in a carriage beside a beautiful, golden-haired maid and people threw flowers in the street before them.

He was the prince.

And he was getting married in a week.

Edward fell ill the next day. He did not come to let her out of her cell. The first two days of isolation weren’t bad. The third day, the snitch’s body began to smell. The fourth day, she tried to feed off it again and gagged. There had not been much in him to begin with, and whatever was left in him now was gelled and rancid. The fifth day, she began to shake. She pounded on the door and the walls and the window until the skin of her fists shed. The sixth day, she began to scream. It came out of her as a long, keening wail. It echoed her hunger, her desperation, her emptiness. Her voice gave out as the sun rose on the seventh day, his wedding day.

She spent the hours curled up against the door, hoping to hear something. Any sign of movement at all would have been welcome. She played with the ends of her faded hair, teasing them in and out between her toes. The shadows moved, lengthened, and eventually, the sun's light died. Her hopes went right along with it. She placed her palm flat on the door beside her head.

It was warm.

She closed her eyes and could feel the energy radiating from the other side. She could hear small, shallow breaths. She could taste sugar on the air.

Molly.

She knocked two times on the door.

"Rose?" the tiny voice called hesitantly.

She knocked two times again.

"Daddy's sick and he had to go away." Skirts rustled against the floorboards. "I'm lonely. Are you lonely?"

Two knocks.

"Do you want to play with my dolly?"

She spread her fingers against the door. "Yeth," she croaked.

The warmth faded, and there were sounds of a heavy chair being dragged across the floor. One, two, three, for, five, six, seven keys were all slowly turned in their locks. The chair was pushed aside, and the door opened.

Molly flew into her arms, the momentum pushing her back onto the bed in her weakened state. She cradled the frightened child in her arms, felt the porcelain head of her dolly poking into her side.

She soaked up the child's energy, willing it into her empty body. She bent her head and smelled the sweetness of her. She nuzzled her nose in the softness of her, like burrowing into the petals of a newly-opened flower.

She shouldn't. She knew she shouldn't, but he had caused her so much pain, and she had nothing left to lose.

Molly screamed and fought, but every bit of her gave the Siren the strength to hold her down, to fill the abyss inside her with this soul of pure innocence. It was so beautiful. The sensations did not wait until she was finished. They exploded into her mind every second. There was fear, yes, sweet fear, but then came sadness and betrayal. There was happiness and laugher, anger and tears, but most importantly, she finally realized the whys. She knew why a person felt joy and why they felt pain. She learned the elation of seeing something for the very first time, and the despair in losing it.

Loss. She knew now what she had been dealing out all this time. There was no way she could have ever known the impact of death without knowing what it was like to live a life. The weight of all the souls she had consumed pressed heavily upon her. She learned consequences. She realized that the things she did affected people other than the person she was killing. She understood that all the pain she had felt before was nothing to the pain these people would feel for the rest of their lives. She felt regret, and love.

Love.

It spread through her. Unconditional love tickled her down to the red tips of her fingers and toes. Love was trust. Love was faith.

Love was believing in the impossible. The rainbow of Molly's soul filled her with love until the last drop. She held Molly's limp body in her arms...and she laughed.

She laughed and laughed, her voice echoing through the dark, vacant house. She laughed until she cried, tears flowing unchecked down her cheeks. She cried for Molly, for all of them. She cried for all the things she had done. She cried for herself, for everything she had lost, for nothing.

Or was it nothing?

She had to hurry. She had to leave this place and never come back. She gently laid Molly's body out on the bed and curled her arm around her dolly. She smoothed back the dark curls and kissed her forehead. She covered herself in the black cloak and fled into the night.

She was glad again to be in the air and running over the earth, despite what little support they gave her. She followed her heart and the dim memories of the snitch up to the castle gates.

She strode up to the guards there and threw her hood back. Those that knew of her let her pass. Those that didn't know of her learned.

The myriad halls and stairs and rooms made the castle a giant labyrinth, but she knew where she was going. Up and up and up...to the balcony suites of the Prince's bedchamber. She did not stop until she was at the foot of his bed, staring down at his sleeping body. She wanted to shake him awake, wanted to explain everything to him, wanted to scream her love for him to the rafters.

But she couldn't.

If he awoke now, he would know what she had become. He would see the evil inside of her, the mark of it in her hair and on her skin. She had saved his life, true, but how many others had she taken on her path back to him? With love came regret. She knew what she had to do. She knew that the only thing she had to offer him now was her absence. If she could just touch him one more time...she reached out a hand to him and stopped herself.

No.

It would not stop at a touch, she knew that from what had happened with Molly. She could never be with him, truly be with him, because eventually she would consume him. His soul was not bright enough for her to survive alone outside it, nor was it strong enough to sustain him once she had consumed it. If she stayed beside him, it would mean his death.

She was a monster.

She forced her hand back to herself and placed it over her heart. She hoped that it spoke enough in the silence for him to hear it, to feel how much she loved him. If it had been water and not air between them, she knew he would have felt it.

He stirred and opened his eyes.

She gave herself one moment, one tiny, blessed moment of looking into his eyes before she turned and ran.

She tripped down the stairs and cut her feet on the stones. The cloak caught on something and she unfastened it. She was sure that soon they would come for her. They would hunt her like the beast she was. She tasted the tears that streamed down her face and knew there was only one refuge.

The cold beach sand kissed her feet like a prayer. The salty spray mixed with her tears, chasing them away. The first tiny wave reached up and licked her toes. Waves rumbled in a cadence she had almost forgotten how to translate.

Come, they pulled.

Home, they crashed.

She took small steps forward. The sand slipped out from beneath her if she stayed too long. The force of the waves pushed her backwards in opposition to the call she felt.

Come, they pulled.

She stumbled, and the tide ripped her sideways along the beach. Gasping, she managed to regain her footing and continue walking out to sea. The current grabbed at her clothes, and she tore them off. The tips of her hair mingled with the foam. Flotsam swirled around her waist.

Home, they crashed.

She walked until the undertow took her and dragged her out to sea.

I lost her sometime before that, back when the moon shone off her white skin and blood red hair. But I didn't have to live inside her anymore to know where she was headed.

She would grab the first sharp object she found – maybe a crab's claw or a clam's shell – and rip gills into herself so that the water could flow through her again. The first one might have been straight, but the rest would be ragged and flawed. She would make her way to the Deep, her body drawn to the neverending call of the soul of the world. She would make a home there among the bloodworms and the warm vents and the other predators.

She would take her love and regret with her. She would heal in the balm of the ocean, away from the complexities of mortal life. She would tell herself that if the day came, if the words were spoken and the magic came to her, she would turn them away. She would not let evil back into the world. The suffering would end with her. She would stew in the self-affliction until it became a dim memory, tucked away in the recesses of her mind like sight and sound, air and fire. Time would fade her lover's face, his name into nothing, and then time itself would melt into darkness. She would ebb and flow and never die.

And when that day did come, ages and ages from now, she would choose the light. She would choose the escape. She would let the evil out one last time just to feel it all again, to live.

As I had.

Strong arms wrapped around me, brushing my satin bedclothes against the small jagged scars on either side of my chest. I leaned back against him, feeling his heartbeat through his chest.

"I just had the strangest dream," he said. I felt his deep voice rumble through the skin of my back. "You came to me while I lay in bed, only your hair was red and your skin was different. You stared at me like you wanted to say something, and then you ran. You looked so...sad."

He turned me around to face him. "The day you saved me was the happiest day of my life. And this day should be the happiest day of yours. Don't be sad."

I smiled and shook my head.

"Good." He kissed me then, long and slow and deep. He hugged me tightly before pulling away. "Come back to bed?"

"Yeth," I whispered, the words still foreign to my tongue. He kissed me once more and left me. I looked out over the moonlit water once more and said my goodbyes before following him, my prince, my soulmate, my love.

Love.

It was the reason I lived.

Well-Behaved Mermaids Rarely Make Fairy Tales

Every mermaid's mother warned against the dangers of rescuing humans. Obviously had Nerissa's mother ever attempted such a thing, she would have mentioned the smell. Men stank of sun, fire, earth and something that made Nerissa's scales crawl. They were heavy, too, not made for swimming, for all that they splashed around madly in the surf like they were. And all that strange raspy breathing!

Thankfully, seawater seemed to stop their bleeding quickly.

Nerissa stared at the fiery wreckage of his ship still aflame on the horizon. The man in her arms was the spitting image of the one from her dreams...minus the webbing between his fingers and the fins...and the inner eyelid. Waking, he stared up at her with eyes as blue as the sky.

"I love you," he said with foul breath. He clutched at her black tresses, limp now in the dry air.

Nerissa could not return to the waves fast enough. From now on, she would listen to her mother. She would never speak of this event. And should she ever again be tempted back to these jagged rocks…well…there were always more humans on the sea.

Blood from Stone

He had no idea that I loved him. He barely acknowledged that I existed, a maid twice over, little more than a shadow in empty hallways. Trapped in unhappy marriage and prisoner in his own castle, he did not conceive that anyone loving him was even possible. The baron was a man of war, not of love.

He was also an ass, but like Maman said, so many men are.

He'd borne arms with Jeanne d'Arc in Orléans, had witnessed firsthand the divine power she had wielded. *Sorceress*, they'd called her. Maman had shared a similar fate, for far less a magical offense.

The baron was so much more deserving of that power. If there existed a man with more confidence, more passion about things beyond the realms of heaven and earth, I never knew of him. Prelati was a pompous, hand waving fool in comparison.

After testing the limits of his seemingly boundless wealth and ultimately finding it, the baron surrounded himself with books and candles and crucifixes in his barren estate, refusing to believe that divine voices could only be heard by the ears of unspoiled females. Yes, it was Prelati who suggested that he was imploring the wrong deity, but it was I who sent him the first child.

"Perhaps those among the fallen might better relate to the sons of Adam."

Prelati's silver-tongued accent echoed through the chimney from which I swept the ashes. The charlatan must have been standing directly in front of the fireplace in the baron's study for his words to have landed so crisply in my unspoiled ears.

I heard the baron's response, rumbled deep from his strong chest, but I did not catch the words. His tone asked a question.

"I will consult my books," replied Prelati, just as he always did. Hidden as I was, I couldn't resist rolling my eyes. Prelati made a far better librarian than an alchemist, or a sorcerer, or a demon-speaker, or whatever color the robes he was wearing today suggested.

Too curious to be privy to half the conversation, I tripped over the ash pail and tore through the cloud of dust out the door and down the hall, hoping to better eavesdrop at the seam between the sitting room doors.

The doors were open.

"I don't care which one, Prelati. Choose whomever—or whatever—you want. I just want some sort of answer, angel or demon or otherwise. There is a way to escape this place, and I will find it. Henriette! You read my mind. Stoke the fire, girl, there's a bit of a chill."

The room was dark; Prelati's idiot form blocked what little light escaped from the dying fire, casting giant shadows of him against the walls hung with thick velvet tapestries to keep out the stones' cold. The air was bitter with the unnatural balsamic tang of Prelati's infernal frankincense.

Prelati scowled at me beneath his great beard and mustaches, so black and thick that he might topple over at any moment with the weight of them. I scowled right back. I didn't care what Prelati thought of me, and he knew it. I worried more that the baron might see an ash smudge upon my cheek, though I was of less note to him than a pebble in his shoe. He ordered me about in the same breath he spoke of summoning demons. I was neither a benefit nor a threat to him and his situation, and he was a skunk for thinking it.

Lord Polecat.

I quickly knelt on the marble hearth, so that only the fire witnessed my grin. I dutifully shoveled the white and gray ashes into the almost full metal bin—the baron often spent long hours in this study, and I was not usually permitted to attend to the fire while his lordship was present. I'd make sure to carry this one away with me when I departed and replace it with the now-empty bin I'd knocked over in the adjacent room. I considered hiding it from cook for a few days before she set me to making the lye soap again.

"We will need candles, my lord, and soft chalk," said Prelati. "If you will excuse me, I will prepare a few new scents that might persuade more unlikely visitors."

I stifled another grin. They'd have to scrape the bottom of the barrel to summon anything more unlikeable than Prelati. My father might have met that criteria, so it's just as well I'm a bastard child. Perhaps I could persuade the baron that my sire had been a demon; he'd have no choice but to notice me then!

I moved quickly across the room with the quiet grace all servants practiced, allowing not so much as a clank from the exceptionally heavy ash bin. Prelati rattled on about his needs and preparations. I dropped a small curtsey to no one and turned.

"Henriette, please send for Poitou; I need the carpets in this study removed."

My breath caught, my chest ached, and my heart skipped a beat at the sound of his voice and the thrill of being addressed, if not seen.

"Yes, sir," I said politely. I curtseyed again and jauntily swung the metal down the cold, dank hall.

I already had plans to make a far more lasting impression.

Unnoticed in plain sight, I monitored their progress for weeks. Every time I crossed the room I skipped and hopped over more and more shapes drawn across the marble. What the baron lacked in funds, it appeared he did not make up for in artistic ability. The air, thick with Prelati's incense experimentation, went from spicy to sweet to cloying; I wondered if he'd begun urinating in the thurible as a last resort.

I continued to empty the ashes from the fireplace while the room was unoccupied, an ever-dwindling window of time in the wee hours of the morning while the men pursued their supernatural prey. Spell after spell failed. I collected my ashes and waited. The morning finally came when the study door was locked, barring me from entrance. Beyond I heard the baron's frustrated, sleep-deprived tones berating Prelati for their constant failure.

It was time.

I excused myself from the palace with a message to Cook that I was to run an errand for the baron. I did not speak untruth—the errand *was* for him, every thought in my head was for him. I covered my hair with a scarf, took a woven basket—so much lighter than ash pails—and walked briskly down the hill into town. The smile never left my face and there was no chill for me that day. The angels had heard my prayers. Patience would deliver me my true love's heart.

I did not have an appointment, but I did not expect to see the furrier himself. "I am sorry, *mademoiselle*," said the furrier's very new and very young apprentice. "But if it is for the baron, perhaps the master will not mind if I go to him."

Brave child; he looked frightened to death at the prospect of disturbing his master at work. I tried to put him at ease. "What is your name, *cherie*?"

"Jeudon, *mademoiselle*."

"Jeudon," I smiled. "It is my own fault for arriving unannounced! I do not think we need to bother your master with this. In fact, I think you might be the perfect person for this job." *Angels, hear my prayers.*

It worked. Jeudon's shoulders relaxed. "Anything at all, *mademoiselle*. For the baron."

"For the baron. Of course! Thank you, Jeudon. But first, I will need to see a sample of your work. I trust your master has started your training on smaller animals, *n'est-ce pas*?"

"*Oui, mademoiselle*. Squirrels and rabbits and the like."

"I don't suppose you've experimented with skunk? Polecat?"

Jeudon's silence at my request answered the question, but I waited him out with a grin.

"*Mademoiselle*, I would never... For the baron..."

"I insist, dear Jeudon! Take me at my word; the baron will be ever-so-impressed that you have such a unique specimen on hand." I reached into my apron pocket, removing seven small pennies—my meager life savings—and I sent up another prayer to those mysterious angels. "Please deliver the fur yourself. This is for your trouble."

"Me, mademoiselle?"

"Yes, please, Jeudon. The baron will want to both pay you and thank you in person. I suggest you make haste!"

The boy did not think twice before rushing into the workroom and scampering out the door with no less than three small pelts in his hand. He left no word for his master, written or otherwise. Just as well. It might be days before anyone discovered he was missing.

Assuming, of course, that the baron understood my gift to him, but I trusted my beloved implicitly.

I spent the next few days making ash soap in the stench-ridden bowels of the castle. It didn't go unnoticed that every room in the castle but the study had lain unused for a month's time. Cook had taken me to task for idling in hallways and banished me thence. The rough, oversized gloves scratched at my knuckles, raw from the cruel ministrations of her wooden spoon, but as not wearing gloves would have been a worse punishment, I bore the pain. I slowly lowered an egg into the still-warm pot of lye, fresh from the fire.

"The baron's called for you."

Cook's announcement from the doorway startled me, and I unceremoniously dropped the egg into the pot, splashing droplets upon my gloves. The egg sank below the surface. I yanked my hand back, pulled the glove off, and fished the egg out with my long-handled spoon. The egg should have bobbed back to the top—this pot would need a bit more time on the fire. But not right now.

I nodded, curtseyed, and slipped beneath Cook's hefty bosom that barred the doorway. I forced my feet to slow, but my heart was flying. I wonder if he'd said my name again, out loud, with those perfect lips, or if he'd just sent a message through Poitou for "the girl who cleans the fireplace." No matter. The baron needed me, far more than he realized.

A full bin of ashes met me outside the study door, so I fetched the empty bin from an adjacent room before knocking on the door.

"Enter."

Oh, if only you would let me. But I dared not meet his eyes. Did he suspect I'd sent the boy? "I'm here for the ashes, my lord." I bent my knees, crossed the room to the fireplace, and stopped dead at a sight I'd never thought I'd see: Prelati on his hands and knees with a scrub brush and bucket.

My hand was too late to hide the smile that betrayed me. Palm firmly clamped over mouth, I skirted around the magician and threw myself down at the hearth. The fire was naught but embers now, but it had burned hot and high and left the ash white. It was also slightly greasy and smelled faintly of brimstone.

Dear, dear Jeudon, I thought, as I shoveled him into my bin. The lard in the mix would undoubtedly make a finer soap. I was too busy wondering how to sneak a batch aside for myself to notice that the room behind me had gone silent. No whispers, no movement, nothing...which could only mean that I was suddenly the center of their attention. I stood tall and dusted my clothes off the best I could before turning to face the two men, both standing now.

The baron was looking at me.

Prelati's gaze slipped to the spot where he'd been scrubbing, and my eyes followed. No doubt they had finally discovered the lengths to which their artistic talent did not go, and chosen to erase the chalk and charcoal and start afresh. True, the lines had been erased, but beneath remained a large, pale pink stain on the perfect white marble.

There was only one thing that stain could be: blood. What would they do with me now that I'd seen it? The baron stared with those intensely hard eyes, sizing me up. I raised my chin and stared right back.

"Do you ever wash floors?" he asked.

"I make the soap," I boasted.

"Have this floor clean by sundown, and we will never speak of this again."

"Yes, my lord." I bent my knees again, collected both ash bins, and went belowstairs to retrieve the soap I'd been stockpiling for this very occasion. I'd considered pocketing some in my apron in preparation for this summons, but I didn't want to play my hand too soon.

Charming, how completely predictable the baron was. But like Maman said, so many men are.

I returned with soap, gloves, and a pot to warm water over the fresh fire I'd built up. I crumbled the lye into powder and set hard to the brush, careful not to get anything on my skin or clothes. It was no easy task, and not quickly done, but before sunset I'd removed every trace of blood from that stone. I stopped on the way back to my rooms only long enough to ask a scrawny young thing to replenish the wood in the baron's study. I didn't bother asking his name.

It was several more days before I was shoveling his ashes out of the fireplace and scrubbing the study floor again. I worked privately and efficiently. As promised, the baron said nothing of the matter.

The third time the baron sent for me, I brazenly spoke without being addressed. "I will clean this floor for you, but I want something."

"We let you keep your life," prattled Prelati. "What more could you possibly desire?"

"In order to properly remove a stain, it's best to catch it right away." My eyes never left the baron's. He knew what I meant.

Or did he? His eyes left mine long enough to gauge Prelati's reaction to my comment.

"Your services are no longer required, girl." Prelati put a hand on the small of my back to lead me to the door and I slapped it away.

I turned to the baron and bowed deeply, in the manner of a *chevalier* and not a scullery maid. My heart beat like a battle drum. "As you wish, Lord Polecat. You may fetch your own errand boys from now on."

I straightened, expecting to see a sly grin upon his countenance with the realization that it was I who'd sent the fitch. What met me instead was a drawn mouth and furrowed brow. I admit I was a little disappointed that such an admirable man like the baron could be so stupid. But like Maman said, so many men are.

Heart in my feet now, I moved to walk away. The bin felt twice as heavy, its scorched refuse now burdened with the leaden weight of my shattered dreams.

"I will do anything."

The baron's voice was low enough to almost be unheard above the crackling of the fresh blaze in the hearth. "I will stop at nothing to regain my fortune, my power, and be free from this place. I will defile heaven and pull demons out of Hell to do my bidding. If you get in my way, I will kill you."

I did not turn back at his words, but I did straighten. The ash bin suddenly felt lighter. "I accept those terms" was all I said before leaving the study.

The next time the baron "sent for a messenger," I accompanied him into the study…and stayed.

Those next few years were the happiest times of my life. Instead of letting our failed attempts at summoning get the best of us, we made a game of it. We gathered young boys from far and wide, for a variety of reasons, and never raised so much as an eyebrow of suspicion. We sometimes drew it out for days, seducing the boys with lavish feasts and mulled wine and games. The baron was pleased to discover that I had a steady hand at runes, despite the hard calluses I earned from scrubbing and soap making. I drew many a circle and lit many a candle. Sometimes we let the boy draw and light them himself. We would stoke the fire high and keep it hot. We always burned the clothes first.

Over time, I even came to tolerate Prelati. It was never anything so bold as "friendship," but we knew each other for what we were, and we each respected the other's loyalty to the baron. Prelati saw that I was a quick study and taught me to read so that I might continue their conversation with new ideas and a fresh perspective. After months of watching me soak ashes in rainwater and strain liquid and boil lye, he invited me to experiment with his incense. I, in turn, taught them both the rudiments of soap making. The baron had a deft hand at floating eggs. I imagined those strong, careful hands on my body many, many more times than I'd like to confess. And the marble was so much easier to clean when we could pour the hot lye right down onto the fresh stain.

I did not let the baron touch me intimately, though I knew at times he wanted to. It was a rush to have such power in one's hands, to literally feel lifeblood slipping from between one's fingers. I drew my best work in that blood. We cleaned the middle of the floor so well and often that I was eventually forced to scrub the rest of the study to match.

Our efforts were not entirely unsuccessful; otherwise, we wouldn't have wasted so much time. There were days when the candles' flame changed color, or the air filled with tiny starbursts of light. Some chants brought a wind that left the room in complete darkness. One even made it rain indoors—I ran so much that day saving the ash pots and collecting fresh water that I fell asleep in wet clothes on the wet settee and did not wake until the next afternoon. Certain chants made the incense smell strongly of roses, or rot. The flavor of everything we ate on those days was wrong. Not always *bad*, mind you, but roast duck that tastes of chocolate pudding is a shock to any palate.

We celebrated our little triumphs. We danced barefoot in the blood, painted ourselves with red and black and white, finished off the mulled wine and sang every silly song we knew until we'd exhausted our repertoire. Then we pulled on our bootstraps, divined what we could from the entrails, added to Prelati's endless stack of notes, and cleared the stage for the next attempt.

I began to dread the day we actually summoned a demon, when I would lose my place in this exclusive club, and lose the baron altogether. *My* baron. We were close to success; I knew it. I could hear it on the wind. I could taste it in the spiced air. I could feel it in my bones. I feared it so much that I finally let him kiss me.

"Let me in," the words were soft, growled into my neck in frustration. My toes slipped in the blood beneath our feet, but I held my ground.

"Make me your wife," I whispered back.

"I have a wife," he said, and not kindly.

I placed my palm flat on his wide chest, leaving a small red print on the white silk. "Your title is married to her. Not your heart."

The next day, he stole us a cleric.

I took an inordinate amount of time preparing for the ceremony. I believe that Prelati deduced my plans—he was smarter than I'd previously given him credit for, especially with regard to subterfuge and mental manipulation—but he said nothing. He mixed the incense concoction we'd agreed upon and painted my face and arms with the necessary symbols after I'd baptized myself in rainwater.

We exchanged gifts, the baron and I, as per tradition more than as a requirement of the summoning ceremony. I gave him a waxen dolly in his own image, as Maman had taught me to do in life, and then taught me never to do again with her death. From my baron bridegroom I received a solid white egg…that I almost dropped when he placed it in my hands. Upon further examination, I realized it was fashioned out of pure white marble—the perfect symbol of the birth of our love for each other. I slipped it into the pocket of my dress so that no blood would mar its pristine surface.

We built up the fire and lit the candles, and when all was ready, Prelati untied the cleric.

The wise man must have realized his fate, for he did not rush the ceremony. My girlish sensibilities thanked him for every extra moment I was allowed to stand upon the symbols with my beloved's hand in mine.

"Lady Polecat," the baron's breath said into mine.

"Lord Fitcher," I replied.

The second time the baron kissed me, I was his wife. Not his first wife on paper, warden to his prison cell, but the first wife in the way that really mattered: the wife of his heart and soul. This love—our love—was true.

But for all the romance I was a practical young girl. I knew that this union did not exist outside this study, or this castle, or even before the cleric's god. We could lie together as man and wife, but that's exactly what it was: a lie. I could lie beside him for the rest of his days and watch him attempt to summon demon after demon until he killed everyone in the castle, and then Prelati, and then himself. Or I could give him what he wanted—what he needed—and set him free.

In my mind, there was never a choice.

Prelati handed the ebony-handled athame to the baron, but this time those beady black eyes never left mine. My love, my *husband*, drew the blade across his palm with a hiss. I took the dagger myself and did the same without so much as exhaling—I could risk losing neither his belief nor his pride in me for the next few moments. We clasped hands with the strength of two lovers facing the universe.

The candles' flames at the points of the star we'd sketched on the marble turned blue and, as before, the air filled with tiny points of light. The fireplace roared, and the thurible's smoke changed from sandalwood to rosemary. The cleric crossed himself. Thrice.

"It's working," the baron said without breathing, as if he might break the spell with a word. "Henriette, my love, it's working!" I would never tire of hearing my name spoken from those lips.

"I know." I tried to reply without gasping, but my body betrayed me. The baron tore his attention away from the magical room to see the dagger in my hand so covered in blood that it totally obscured the double blade. My virgin bride's blood dripped from my core onto the rune-riddled marble between us.

My true love held me in strong arms; had my silly girlish legs not already given way, they would have then. "What have you done?" He might have screamed this, but I only heard him whisper.

"Freed you," I said, or perhaps I said. Perhaps the only fragment to escape my lips had been "free," but that syllable conveyed the message just as well.

There was no blackness for me to succumb to, nor was there a legendary white light for me to follow. The room stayed exactly as it was, in stark detail, and I tried to commit as much to memory as I could before one entity or another whisked me away to some great beyond. The baron knelt over my limp body, repeating "No" over and over again as if the chant might act as a tether to pull my soul back into my body. Prelati stood to one side of the circle in his solemn violet robes and bowed his head, praying to…something. So neither one of them saw the portal open and the man in black step through.

The man was followed by two angels, both terrible, one with wings of feathers and one with wings of fire. My sacrifice had not summoned a demon, then, it had summoned a *god*. This could only be Lord Death himself.

"We seem to have ourselves a dilemma."

Awestruck, Prelati fell to his knees beside the baron. The cleric passed out cold.

"Bring back my wife." The baron did not implore Lord Death

so much as order him to do so.

"See, that's just the thing." Lord Death crossed his legs and sat on the stone casually before them, before my dead body. The angels remained standing, one to either side of him, as did my ethereal soul. Exactly how much of the room's population could the baron and Prelati see?

"What your loving 'wife' has done here is sacrifice herself for you," Lord Death continued. "To bring her back would undo all that precious magic you've managed to accomplish."

The baron did not reply, but Prelati nodded.

"This girl has made you capable of *love*, of all things. She's also, in one fell swoop, stopped you from ever killing another child again. Am I right?"

The baron gave the idea some thought before nodding his own assent. Of course my love would no longer bother himself with children. The key to his prison had been there all along in the very thing he eschewed: divinity still had a soft spot for unspoiled females. The marriage ceremony had caught their attention, and the blood had kept it.

"I must honor this sacrifice, as much as it pains me to do so." Lord Death scanned the room, from the well-scrubbed floor to the cinder-strewn hearth. The angel of fire's wings burned ever brighter, and I choked on her ash.

The baron—my baron—took up the bloody athame and looked to a sky that was not there. "Then let me follow her."

Lord Death stayed his hand. "Yeah, let me stop you right there. See, if you do that now, it's not a sacrifice. It's suicide. That particular end will deliver you to a very different place. Am I right?" This was directed at the cleric who, having come to, nodded vigorously. "You will never join her, my dear baron, until you die by a hand other than your own. A death that serves to free the soul of someone else."

The baron looked to Prelati, who raised his own hands in defeat. Prelati's soul was well beyond saving.

"Please," said the baron, and it was a tone I had only ever heard him use to me. "Let her stay with me. There must be some way. Let her haunt me until the end of my days, if you must, but let her stay with me."

"I'm inclined to agree, actually," said Lord Death. "It would be a fitting end for both of you." He gestured to the angel of feathers and that bright light I'd heard so much about finally washed over me. There was a rush of wind and a choir of springtime. I felt blood in my veins and breath in my lungs and strength in my sinew. When my vision cleared, I was viewing the scene from a very new perspective, right in front of Lord Death's face. I screamed, and the dim study echoed with birdsong.

I had wings, indeed, but I was no angel.

"She will stay with you, as requested, until you are relieved of your earthly, fleshy prison." Lord Death stood. "You deserve each other." That mystic portal appeared again, and the angels of feathers and fire sped through the opening before him. Lord Death was halfway through before he turned back for one last remark.

"Oh. And Prelati—cut it out, already."

"Yes, my lord." They were the last words the magician said

before they both disappeared.

Overwhelmed, the cleric fainted. Again.

My beloved took my earthly body down, down, down to my rooms in the bowels of his castle, where no one ever saw me but the fire and the ashes and Cook. I fluttered after him on awkward wings. He laid my body on the table: black hair, white dress, red blood and all. He spent a very long time arranging my limbs and clothes. I used the time to find currents of air around the room, getting used to my new body. When he was satisfied he banked the fire, closed the door to the room, and locked it tight.

He slid the key onto the chain around his neck that once bore a cross—now it held our wedding bands. He pressed his forehead against the door and whispered something, but I didn't catch it. In his hands—larger to me now than they ever had been—was a small white object. My bride gift. He must have rescued it from my pocket when he'd been arranging my dress! My rapidly beating little heart swelled with pride and I burst into song.

The baron raised the perfect white egg to his lips and kissed it, as he had once kissed me. "We have lots of work ahead of us, little bird. There's a floor in my study that needs scrubbing." I perched on his outstretched hand and he stroked my feathers with fingers that would be forced to draw new runes and symbols all on their clumsy own. "And then…let's find a new wife!"

Unicorn Gold

Once upon a time, there lived a selfish young prince who was very bored. Moping about his castle one day, he overheard two men talking about a unicorn in the Wood. Unicorns were the most beautiful creatures in all the land, with hide like clouds and hair like rain and eyes like love, but they were swift and nigh impossible to catch. The only way anyone might capture one was with a harness of gold, fashioned by the hunter's own hand.

Suddenly, the prince wanted a unicorn more than anything in the world.

Knowing that he could not ask his father to fund his quest, he brought a small chest of what gold coins he had down to the smithy. The prince promised a third of the finished product for teaching him how to make the harness.

"It is not enough gold, highness," said the smith. "Then I shall borrow some," said the prince. And so he did. But his friends were all as selfish as he, and they did not spare much.

"It is not enough gold, highness," said the smith. "Then I shall beg for some," said the prince. And so he did, dressing in vagrant's robes and shaking a cup in the streets. But his subjects were all as selfish as he, and they did not spare much.

"It is still not enough gold, highness," said the smith. "Then I shall steal some," said the prince. And so he did, creeping into the jeweler's shop late at night and selecting the finest golden wares. But this jeweler was no ordinary shopkeep; he was a fairy who magicked his wares. The night after a theft, every bit of stolen gold, and any other gold kept beside it, would find its way back to its rightful owner.

Ignorant of the curse, the prince brought his bounty to the smith, who finally proclaimed it enough. By midday he was done his hammering, by late afternoon he wandered the Wood, and by dusk he was tired enough to rest his weary bones against the trunk of a sturdy old tree. By nightfall, he was asleep. And as the stars winked into the black heavens, so did the golden harness disappear bit by bit: a third back to the jeweler, a third back to those who had given their charity, and a third to the coffers of the patient smith for payment.

When the unicorn woke him, the prince stared up at her gleaming horn, her skin like clouds, her hair like wind, and her eyes like love. She smelled like mist and whispers. She felt like peace and home. She stood right there before him, and he had nothing to hold her.

"Silly, selfish prince," said the unicorn. "There was never a harness made of metal that could capture me. It is only gold from the heart which binds me." She laid her gleaming horn upon his breast. "Had you fashioned a harness from what lay in here, you might have had me." She lifted her head. "A false heart never won true love."

And then she was gone.

Sunday

y name is Sunday Woodcutter, and I'm ungrateful.

I am the seventh daughter of Jack and Seven Woodcutter, Jack a seventh son and Seven a seventh daughter herself. Papa's goal in life was to give birth to the charmed, all-powerful, much-talked-about Seventh Son of a Seventh Son. Mama told him she had just enough in her for seven girls or seven boys, but not both. Papa was sure his dream would come true when Jack Junior was the first of us to introduce himself to the world. That dream died the morning I popped out - eight children later - and Mama declared her womb officially closed for business.

I never knew Jack Junior, but I know his legend. I grew up surrounded by overdramatic songs and stories of his exploits and adventures, a good number of which continue to pop up about the countryside to this very day. At a very young age, I decided that the truth about him laid in the pauses between the sagas and the stanzas, in those brief moments when a man is still a man and not a mountain. The silence paints a picture of a handsome, hotheaded youth of too many words and too few thoughts to precede them. One thought more might have stopped my eldest brother before he killed young Prince Rumbold's prize watchdog; one word less and he might not have goaded the prince's evil father into siccing the prince's eviler fairy godmother on him. Jack Junior was witched into a dog and forced to work in the slain mutt's stead forevermore.

For fifteen long years my father has dutifully paid the family's tax and tithe; and despite the fact that he harbors no loyalty to the royal family whatsoever, Papa wisely never says a word against them. As the unhappy incident happened the year before I was born – with the whole of my family alive at the time save me – I have always felt entirely left out of the matter.

My second eldest brother's name is Jack as well, but we call him Jackie. The youngest's name is Trix – which everyone assumes simply stands for "Jack Number Three." They would be wrong of course, but none of us has ever felt compelled to correct them. Trix was a foundling child that Papa discovered in the limbs of a tree at the edge of the forest one winter's workday. Mama says she was resigned to the fact that since she already had eight children to feed, what was one more or less? I have a feeling I know the truth of that too. Attached to Mama's swift hand for discipline is the heart of a compassionate woman who could not abandon a child in the Wood, no matter how fey his origin.

My sisters and I—

"What are you doing?"

Sunday's head snapped up from her book, her heart fell into her stomach, and every hair on her arms stood on end. She had chosen this spot for its solitude, followed the half-hidden path through the underbrush to the decaying rocks of the abandoned well, sure that she had escaped from her family. And yet the voice that had interrupted her thoughts was not familiar to her.

Her eyes took a moment to adjust, slowly focusing in on the mottled shadows that the afternoon sun cast through the dancing leaves of the trees above.

"I'm sorry?" She posed the polite query to her unknown visitor in an effort to make him reveal himself, be he real or imagined, dead or alive, fairy or...

"I said, 'What are you doing?'"

...frog.

It took Sunday a second to make her gaping mouth form words that made sense. "I'm..." All caught off guard like that, she found herself sputtering the truth. "Telling myself stories."

"Why? Do you have no one to whom you can tell them?"

It took her another second. "Well, no...I have quite a big family, actually. With lots of stories. Only..."

"Only what?"

"Only no one wants to hear *my* stories. I could tell them, but they wouldn't listen."

"I will listen," said the frog. "Read me your story, the story that you have just written there, and I will listen."

It was completely absurd. Absurd that Sunday was somewhere in the middle of the Wood talking to a frog who wanted her to make him what she desired most in the world: a captive audience to her words. It was so absurd, in fact, that she started reading from the top of the page in her book without another thought.

"'My name is Sunday Woodcutter—'"

"Grumble," croaked the frog.

"If you're going to grumble through the whole thing, why did you ask me to read it in the first place?"

"You said your name was Sunday Woodcutter," said the frog, "and I thought it only fitting to introduce myself in kind. My name is Grumble."

"Oh." Her face felt hot. Sunday wondered briefly if frogs could tell that a human was blushing, or if they were one of the many other colorblind denizens of the forest. "It's very nice to meet you."

"Thank you," said Grumble. "Please, carry on with your story."

She did. It was a little awkward, as Sunday had never before read her musings aloud to anyone. Her voice sounded loud and the words seemed foreign and sometimes wrong; she resisted the urge to change them or scratch them out altogether as she went on. For as long as she had sat under the tree writing them down, they were quickly read and over with in no time at all.

"I had meant to go on about my sisters," Sunday apologized when she got to the end, "but…"

"I interrupted you. Forgive me." Grumble hopped forward onto a closer damp stone. "As you can imagine I don't get many visitors. I thank you for indulging me with your words, kind lady."

"It was an honor," she said automatically.

"Do you write often?"

"Yes. Every morning and every night and every moment I can sneak in between."

"And do you always write about your family?"

Sunday flipped the pages of her neverending journal – a gift from Fairy Godmother Joy – past her thumb. It was a nervous habit she had had all her life. "I do," she admitted, "but only because I am afraid to write anything else."

"Why is that?"

She shifted her legs to a more comfortable position beneath her skirts. "Things I write...well...they have a tendency to come true. And not in the best way."

"You must always be careful what you wish for," said the frog.

"Exactly," nodded Sunday. "So if I only write about events that have already come to pass, then there is no danger of my accidentally altering the future."

"A very practical decision," said Grumble.

"Yes," she sighed. "Very practical and very boring. Very just like me."

"On the contrary. I found your brief essay quite intriguing."

"Really?" The thought occurred to her that he was just saying it to be nice, because it was expected. And then she remembered he was a frog.

"Would you mind coming to read to me again tomorrow? I would love to hear more of the story."

If the smile Sunday knew was currently spread across her face didn't scare him off, surely nothing she wrote could. "I would love to."

"And would you…be my friend?"

The request was so charmingly humble. "Only if you will be mine in return."

Grumble's mouth opened wide into what Sunday took must have been a froggy grin.

"And…if I may be so bold, Miss Woodcutter…" he started.

"Please, call me Sunday."

"Sunday…do you think you could find it in your heart to…kiss me?"

Sunday had wondered how long it would take before he got around to asking. She had assumed from the beginning that he was either a fey-blessed amphibian or an enchanted man, and his overly proper mannerisms had her leaning toward the latter. A maiden's kiss was the usual remedy for that sort of thing. She was actually quite impressed that he had managed to sneak it in during the mere hour of their brief acquaintance. But he had been very polite, and as Sunday was surely the only maiden he would come across for a very long time it was the least she could do.

She placed her hands on the mossy stones of the ruined well and leaned down. His skin was bumpy and slightly wet beneath her lips, but she tried not to think about it.

Nothing happened.

They sat there, staring at each other for a long time afterwards.

"I don't have to come back you know," Sunday told him, "in case you were offering just to be courteous."

"Oh no," he said. "I look forward to hearing about your sisters. Please, do come back tomorrow."

"Then I will, after I finish my chores. But I should be going now, before it gets dark." She stood and brushed what dirt she could off her skirt. "Good night, Grumble."

"Good night, Sunday."

My sisters and I are the unfortunate product of a woman with as little creativity at naming as her mother before her. Jack Junior was definitely his mother's son in this, for had she thought things through Mama might have realized that the naming of her daughters was as clever in its simplicity as it was damning in its curses. Second born to my mother were the twins, thus securing a female majority in the household that was never again in jeopardy.

Monday was indeed fair of face, but Tuesday was the dancer.

I have patchwork memories of a slip of a young woman, a moth at the flame, a vision of constant movement whose grace the reeds and sunsets envied. The epitome of the Life of the Party, Tuesday garnered invitations from Royal Balls to County Fairs. She was loved by all who knew her, both human and fey. Mama enjoyed the popularity but complained about the cost of keeping her active daughter in shoes, which she often remarked was "more than enough for *twelve* dancing princesses." It seemed a godsend to her when an elfin shoemaker gifted Tuesday with a pair of scarlet slippers he swore would never wear out. It turned out to be true, for Tuesday could not dance those shoes to death.

They danced her to death instead.

There was immense sadness in the wake of Tuesday's passing, but no one mourned more than Monday. Once a week, Monday would walk the many miles from our ramshackle cottage in the Wood to the cemetery on the hill and place flowers on her twin's grave. Every Tuesday she went, rain or shine, sleet or snow, despite our parents' wishes. One sickly green morning she went out again, heedless, and on the way home was caught in a storm sent from the bowels of hell itself. Tossed in the wind, pelted by walls of rain and battered by fists of ice, Monday got lost in the Wood on the way back and found herself at the doorstep of a well-kept cabin.

Inside the cabin were two princes on hunting holiday – one dark and one fair - who had chosen to celebrate the storm as some men choose to celebrate everything. The fair prince began to congratulate himself on his recent success at finding a wife – he had given the girl a test and she had passed with flying colors, having spun three rooms full of straw into gold for him. The dark one proclaimed the Wife Test a marvelous idea, and determined that *his* wife would be so delicate that she would not be able to sleep comfortably with a pea under the mattresses. They were well into their cups when Monday arrived, a bedraggled wretch on the doorstep begging asylum.

The next morning, when Monday appeared before them with a rash of fresh bruises from head to toe, the dark prince fell to his knees and asked for her hand in marriage.

We owe our current livelihood to Monday. Her bridegift was a tower at the edge of the Wood that had no door—

"No door?" Grumble croaked in dismay.

"None whatsoever," Sunday said. "If it had ever been part of a castle, that part was long gone. The tower only had a window, and very high up. The property belonged to the prince's grandmother. It had been handed down in the female line for generations, but was never used. We were crawling over ourselves like rats in our little cottage, so Papa knocked a door in the tower and built the rest of the house around the base. Unfortunately, it looks nothing like a castle. More like..." She closed her eyes and remembered the years of schooltime ridicule she had borne. "...a shoe."

"A shoe."

The way he said it made Sunday chuckle despite herself. "Between Tuesday's fate and our house, it seems that shoes are a recurring theme in my life."

"And what of your other sisters?"

Sunday folded her book across her stomach and stretched out in a patch of fading sunlight on the moss-covered ground. "Wednesday is the poet. She's been nicking Fairy Joy's absinthe since she was old enough to hold a pen."

"Fairy Joy?"

"Our godmother." The sun was warm on her weary bones, and the conversation was low and comfortable. Sunday smiled and wished she could stay there forever. "Thursday always had itchy feet. She ran off with a Pirate King when she was about my age, but she still sends us letters and gifts from time to time. Friday is the best of us all, and spends most of her days at the church helping the orphans and the elderly. Saturday is the sturdy, practical one. She goes into the Wood every morning with Papa and Jackie and helps with the cutting."

"And you're ungrateful."

The laugh that burst from Sunday's lips surprised her. It was a curious thing, having one's words thrown back like that. She turned to Grumble and propped her head in one hand. "'Bonny and blithe and good and gay,'" she recited. "Who could live up to that? And even if they could, what sort of tapioca-pudding life would that be? I told Mama I would much prefer an interesting life to a happy one. She called me ungrateful, and so I am."

"And you are a writer, like you sister."

"Well, I'm not quite so melancholy gravy as Wednesday, Our Lady of Perpetual Shadow...but yes, a little in my own way."

"You have a gift for words," said Grumble.

"A curse more like," Sunday sighed. "Mama says I spend too much of my life in little fantasy worlds and not enough time in this one. And speaking of time," the pool of sunlight had long since faded and the night breeze was cool on her skin, "I should be getting back home before I am missed."

"Will you come again tomorrow?" Grumble said as she sat up. "Please?"

"I will try." She ran her fingers through her hair in an effort to dislodge the bits of twigs and grass that had used her head as a playground.

"And...Sunday?"

"Yes?"

"Would you kiss me before you go?"

It hadn't worked yesterday; it would no doubt fail again today. Sunday felt terrible for her new friend. But his little heart held more hope than most people had in a lifetime, and who was she to belittle that? "Of course," she said, and leaned down to kiss his back. "Good night, Grumble."

"Good night, Sunday."

"Grumble? Are you here?" Sunday carefully tiptoed around the crumbled pieces of the well in search of her friend. She knew she was earlier than usual, and she didn't know if Grumble went elsewhere or hid under the well water in the heat of the day. The rocks were perspiring more than Sunday was, and she slipped. She threw her arms out in an effort to catch herself – the last thing she wanted to do was squash the only friend she had – and after tilting about madly for a moment she regained her balance.

There was a deep, rumbling croak to her left. The little scamp was laughing at her!

"Caught that, did you?"

"Yes," he answered, "though I was afraid for a moment you wouldn't."

Sunday sat down on a more level section of ground. "Grace was not my virtue, remember?"

"So true, so true." He hopped closer. "I didn't expect you until later."

"This was the only time I could get away," she told him as she pulled her little book out of her pocket. "I'm supposed to be accompanying Trix to market to sell the cow, which means my chores will no doubt take up the rest of the day."

"Will your brother be all right by himself?"

That wasn't what she was worried about. "He knows exactly where to go, to whom he's supposed to sell the cow, and what price he's to fetch. He'll be fine." Sunday ran her thumb across the pages of the book. "I didn't have time to write anything for you. I'm so sorry."

"I'm sorry too," said Grumble after a moment. "There is something about your stories, your words, your voice. They make me…remember. What it was like to be a man."

She was a terrible friend. How selfish of her to have ever imagined that he asked for her company simply to humor her. "Are you in danger of forgetting?"

"I've already forgotten faces and names," he said forlornly, "my own included. I've forgotten what it's like to get out of bed in the morning. The feel of clothes on my skin. Food. I think I loved food once."

Her heart went out to him.

"When I'm lost in your words," he continued, "I forget that I am a frog. Instead I am just a man, sitting here with his beautiful friend, listening to her tell him about her interesting life. It's a wonderful feeling."

Sunday bit her lip. It was the loveliest thing anyone had ever said to her in her whole entire life.

"I'm afraid you have ruined me, Sunday. I didn't realize how much I longed for the company of others until I had your words.

And when they are gone...the nights are darker without them. The silence is loud and bottomless, and I am empty. I miss them, my beloved Sunday. I miss you."

It was no use fighting. The tears came anyway. She was powerless to break his spell, but she could give him what she had. She opened her book to the next blank page and started writing. When she was done, she leaned back and smiled at her friend. "'Sunday was nothing,'" she read aloud, "'until she met Grumble – a beautiful man, with the soul of a poet. He was her best friend in the whole wide world, and she loved him with all her heart.'" She closed book gently in her lap. "I wish—"

"Sunday!" Her name was yelled loudly, from far away.

Trix? What was he doing back so soon? He should have been gone another hour or two at least.

"Suuuuun-daaaaaay," Trix called through the woods.

"I'm here!" she called back. "Well," she said to Grumble, "like it or not, you're about to meet some of my family."

"It will be an honor," said the frog.

Trix came crashing through the brush and stumbled into the clearing. "Cooooooool," he said breathlessly. "A Fairy Well." For all that he was at least two years her senior, Trix both looked and acted as if he had stopped aging at twelve. Sunday grabbed ahold of his scrawny wrist before he could scamper off across the rocks and break his neck.

"The cow," She reminded him. "You took her to market and sold her that quickly?" It was more of a hope than a question.

Trix's wide grin was unsettling. "I am a lucky tradesman," he announced, “and a shrewd one. I happened upon a man in the woods who was on his way to market for just such a cow.”

Sunday’s heart that had only moments before soared in her chest sank lower and lower with every word that passed Trix’s lips. No. Please, God, no.

“So I sold it to him for these.” He opened his palm so she could see what was inside it.

Her heart plummeted into her feet. She was going to throw up. “Beans.”

“Magic beans,” Trix said proudly. “He was only going to give me one, but I bartered my way up to five. After all, what if one doesn’t sprout? Smart thinking, eh?” Trix tucked the beans back in his pocket and patted them. “I figure I can plant them under my treehouse and…Sunday? Are you okay?”

Sunday had stopped breathing. She was a dead woman. Trix was her responsibility, and she had let him go off alone and trade their best cow for…for…

“Sunday?” Trix was suddenly worried.

“Mama will kill me,” she whispered. “We needed that money, Trixie. How will we eat?”

“You’ll see.” His voice was filled with childish wonder. “My magic beans will grow, and we will have food forever.”

His innocence was as beautiful in its purity as it was frustrating. He didn’t understand, and she didn’t know how to make him. “Beans take time to grow,” Sunday explained. “What will we eat tomorrow? And the next day?”

At least that much seemed to sink in. “I’m sorry, Sunday,” he said quietly. "I don't want you to die."

"If I may be so bold."

In her misery, Sunday had completely forgotten about Grumble. He was sitting patiently beside a perfectly round, slime-covered rock.

"Forgive me. Trix, meet my friend Grumble. Grumble, this is my brother Trix."

"Wow," said Trix.

"Charmed," said Grumble.

"Whatcha got there?" Trix sat down unceremoniously beside Grumble and picked up the spherical stone.

"Something I'm hoping will save your sister's life," he said. "A life that's become uncommonly important to me over the last few days."

Frogs must be colorblind after all, Sunday decided. It was a sweet gesture. To Grumble, the ball must have looked like a precious gem, or a fairy trinket, or...

"Gold!" cried Trix.

"What?" Sunday snatched the ball out of her brother's hand. She was so unprepared for the weight of it, she almost dropped it. She scraped at the scum with her fingernail to the smooth, hard surface beneath. "It is!" She hugged the bauble to her.

And then she remembered that she wasn't a hoarding kobold.

Sunday held the ball back out to Grumble.

"We can't take this."

"Sunday, I'm a frog. What use have I for such a pretty?"

"But its worth alone..."

"That and a hundred more like it wouldn't get me what I want," he reminded her. "But if it buys even a second of your family's happiness, then to me it is worth more than any moneylender could possibly exchange for it."

He was right, she knew. But her conscience still wouldn't let her. Sunday stood there, weighing her needs against her morals.

They both weighed about three pounds of solid gold.

"Please," said Grumble.

Sunday put the bauble in her pocket. She cradled Grumble in her hands and kissed him heartily before he could ask her. "Thank you, my dear friend, more than you will ever know." He was too stunned for words. "Trix and I should be going now," she said. "But I will come back tomorrow. And I will write for you, I promise!"

She did not hear him say goodbye.

Excited, Sunday skipped in Trix's wake back through the brush. They raced each other to the edge of the Wood, to where their house laid on the horizon. Their energy spent, they slowed to a walk, the weight of the golden ball knocking reassuringly between Sunday's book and her leg.

"He loves you."

Trix was like that. Full of snails and puppy dogs' tails one minute, and unnaturally wise the next. What he said was true, but it did not change the way of the world.

"And you love him."

Nor did that.

Sunday covered the lump in her skirt pocket with her hand and said the only thing she could think to say.

"I know."

Sunday awoke to a poke in the side and opened her eyes to see her mother looming over her bed. Seven Woodcutter was not a soft, warm, cookie-making type of mother. She was more of a "spoil the rod" type of mother. At least she wasn't using the rod to wake up her children. Anymore.

Sunday felt the familiar rustle of pages under her cheek. Her family's celebration over their newfound wealth had lasted well into the night, and she had fallen asleep committing the revelry to paper so that she could share it with Grumble in the morning. She knew he would be delighted to hear it.

Her gaze flew to the candlestick beside the bed, and the small stub of candle atop it. Dear, good Friday. She must have come into Sunday's room in the wee hours to snuff it out behind her. Mama always let Sunday have it whenever she discovered a candle burned down to the quick, for it was irrefutable proof that at least some of it had been wasted. Despite the fact that Monday could provide for everything they would ever need, Mama was a penny pincher to the end.

"There's been a Proclamation," Mama said by way of explanation.

Great. Royal Proclamations usually meant more work, less food, and the loss of something they had previously taken for granted.

"Prince Rumbold is hosting three balls."

Prince Rumbold. The prince whose fairy godmother had turned

the brother Sunday had never known into a dog. The prince who had been reported ill or missing or dead or all three over the past several months. The prince who had evidently been restored to health, rescued, resurrected or simply rumored about. Whatever the story, the spirit had apparently moved His Evil Highness to throw a ball. So he was pretentious enough to have three, and then announced them to the countryside like anyone cared a fig.

"Good for Prince Rumbold." Sunday rolled over and buried her face in the pillow, her pillow that smelled deliciously of sleep.

Another poke. "The prince is throwing three balls, and all the eligible ladies in the countryside are invited," Mama said. "If you are very good and do all your chores, I will let you go."

"Perfect," Sunday said into the pillow. "I don't want to go."

She felt the pages of her book slip from beneath her cheek. Sunday reached out to grab it, but Mama was too quick.

"You will go into town and sell that little golden bauble," she ordered. Sunday's eyes never left the book she held hostage; Mama had her rapt attention. "In addition to what we normally use, you will buy all the fabric Friday needs to alter dresses for you girls; she is in the kitchen right now making a list. You will do your chores *and* Friday's for the next three days, and then at the end of them, you will attend those balls."

"What does Papa have to say about all this?" Sunday snapped.

"Your father has no say in this. Every eligible girl in the country has been asked to attend, which means that every eligible man of means will find a way to be invited. I don't care if it is that awful prince's doing. This may be my girls' only chance to snare a decent husband, and they will not pass up that chance. I will see at least one of you engaged before the week is out. Do I make myself clear?"

Sunday nodded silently as Mama slipped the book into her pocket. It would have been impossible for her to not feel Sunday's desperation.

"Sunday," Mama said more easily, "it's not that difficult. Just do what I need you to do, and I will let you have your diary back before you go to bed every night. But I will take it away again every morning, understand?"

"Yes, Mum!" Sunday hopped out of bed, unable to dress and run to market fast enough.

The trip to market was unbelievable. Sunday was treated like a princess from the moment she arrived at the moneylender's office. He had smiled at the bauble and told her that he was going to have to consult with someone about it, but as he did not want to keep her from shopping he gave her tokens with the royal seal on them and instructed her to leave one with each vendor she purchased goods from. After Trix's misfortune she was wary about trading for a handful of anything, but the vendors lit up at the sight of the tokens and made sure to present to her the finest of their wares. She was probably still a little too frugal with her purchases; even though she had to hire a wagon to help her home with them, she still had a small bag full of gold pieces left over.

Once at home she immediately went to work on her chores. Mama was so pleased with her that she handed Sunday her book directly after supper. While Sunday regretted not being able to spend even a moment with her new best friend, she had experienced the entire day with an eye for how she would tell Grumble all about it. He would be so happy to see her, and she would read to him for hours, and he would understand why she hadn't come.

The next two days passed in a blur. The only moments that seemed to drag were the rare occasions that Sunday had to gaze longingly at the treeline of the Wood. She missed her friend more with every hour that she was away, and she hoped he was not desperately pining for her.

Though if her feelings were any judge, he undoubtedly was.

At the end of the third day, Sunday sat in front of the mirror in a gown of silver and tried not to fall asleep while Wednesday braided her hair.

"The words," said Wednesday dreamily. (Wednesday said everything dreamily.) "They're keeping you up at night." If anyone understood the power of words, it was Wednesday.

"Yes," Sunday admitted.

"It shows."

That was less than reassuring.

"But don't worry," her dark sister added. "You look like..." her voice floated off into the ether. She wove a ribbon into the plait. "You still look beautiful."

Papa said nothing as he watched his women climb inside the carriage. He twisted the small gold medallion on the chain around his neck; Sunday had come by her nervous idle hands honestly. She suddenly wished she had her book with her to keep her company.

To give her courage.

Papa had tears in his eyes when he looked at Sunday. She felt miserable. Like she was betraying him by even attending the ball. Like she was betraying Grumble.

Once at the palace they walked up the steps and across the yard to where the gaggle of other women were waiting to be announced at the Grand Entrance. Sunday was sure that the Woodcutter women made an odd picture. Mama was humble in her matronly mauve. Friday almost skipped in her scarlet. Saturday lumbered in her lavender, her flat-footed gait betraying the fact that she hated wearing a dress more than anything in the world, and that she would have preferred a death sentence to what awaited beyond those doors. Wednesday glided, a waif in her fairy-kissed grey, as if she were wearing her own shadow. And Sunday in her silver walked next to them, feeling more the pretender and betrayer with every step that she took.

Sunday didn't realize she had no idea what she was getting into until she walked through the doors of the Grand Entrance and stood on the landing overlooking the ballroom floor.

It was more people than she had ever seen in her life.

Her breath caught in her throat. Her face flushed. Her heart raced. She froze in place, unable to take another step forward. She felt Wednesday's cool hand slip inside her clammy one, and it gave her the courage to move forward to the top of the red-carpeted stairs. She immediately saw herself plummeting down them.

Wednesday squeezed her fingers.

"Missus Seven Woodcutter," the servant announced, "and her

daughters: Miss Wednesday, Miss Friday, Miss Saturday, and Miss Sunday Woodcutter."

Sunday wouldn't have been surprised if the whole room had turned to laugh at their ridiculous names. Thank God there were only four of them. She picked up her skirts in one hand and held fast to Wednesday with the other, letting her sister ease her slowly down the steps.

She was happy to see a familiar face meet them at the bottom, smiling behind a jewel-studded fan.

"Monday," Mama crooned as she embraced her eldest daughter. Sunday's eyes never left the fan. So much nonsense over a stupid cow that wasn't worth half of the useless accessory her sister currently held nonchalantly in her hand. But Mama's pride kept her from taking any charity from Monday, and they were all better off for it. As she reminded them. Daily.

Sunday's princess sister took her hand from Wednesday's and looked her over. Sunday bowed her head in a small curtsey.

"She looks like Tuesday," Monday said to Mama.

Mama turned. Sunday thought it might have been the first time in her life her mother had actually *looked* at her. "She does, a little," Mama said after a pause.

Sunday's racing heart tripped over itself and skipped a beat in the process. It was the nicest thing her mother had ever said to her. The music stopped. The room went quiet. Sunday was too shocked to notice anything, until she realized that her family were staring at a point just to the left of her head. Behind her.

"Miss Woodcutter," he said.

Sunday turned slowly, and uttered the first words that came to mind that were not profane. "Your Highness."

"Would you do me the honor of accompanying me in the next dance?"

From a man like him, it was a rhetorical question. Sunday straightened out of her curtsey and took his hand as he led her to the center of the room. She stared at the gold medal on his breast, afraid to look at him.

She did not think the prince was simply a shallow man with an eye for a pretty face; there were many girls much prettier than she in the room. He must have known of their connection. Even if he had been too young to remember it, surely he must have heard the legend of Jack Junior. Perhaps this was his way of mending ways between their families. Perhaps this was his way of demonstrating that he always got what he wanted. Perhaps this was a display of his complete and utter ignorance.

The band started a waltz.

Oh why me, Sunday repeated to herself with every movement. *Oh why me, oh why me, oh why me*...over and over again as they turned in the sea of beautiful people, over and over again until she slipped and said it aloud.

"Why?" said the prince. "Well, because I needed to ask someone a question, and you looked intelligent enough to answer it honestly."

"As you wish, Your Highness." It was a knee-jerk reaction to curtsey at the title, and Sunday found herself stumbling. The prince spun her around to cover up the misstep.

"My fault," he said quickly. "So, are you ready for my question?"

She nodded sternly.

"Do I look as stupid as I feel?"

Sunday bit her lips together and tried not to laugh. One did not laugh at His Royal Highness. After a count of three, she felt calm enough to reply. "It would not matter if Your Highness was wearing a sackcloth," she said. "Or nothing at all. No one would ever think you looked stupid, and if they did they would not be traitorous enough to say so."

"Exactly," said the prince. "Which is why I am asking you. I think myself a relatively good judge of character, and I have a feeling that you are the type of person who does not lie casually."

"In that case," said Sunday, "you look fine. Very smart. Very handsome. As a prince should look. Although..."

"Tell me."

"There is a bit of your hair sticking out on the left side."

"I knew it!" the prince said through his teeth. "Damn nuisance. There is no help for it."

"I'm sure if you smoothed it down with your hand quickly, no one would notice."

"You said it yourself, Miss Woodcutter. Everyone is looking. Everyone would notice, and they would all say I was too vain for my own good."

"I would do it for you," offered Sunday, "but everyone would say I was too familiar."

The prince threw back his head and laughed loudly. Sunday tensed in his arms as she felt every eye in the room turn to them in wonder. She was instantly reminded of her place in the world.

Perhaps it was a good thing. She had been feeling entirely too comfortable with this man who was supposed to be her enemy. She felt her cheeks turn instantly red, which no doubt sent more tongues wagging.

"I love that you blush."

"Why did you do that?" Sunday whispered.

"Because everyone was looking," he said, "and now everyone is gossiping. Everyone already assumes that you are too familiar, so you must dance every dance with me after this. And in order to save yourself the humiliation of being seen dancing with a lunatic all night, you have no choice but to fix my hair."

He smiled in triumph.

"Scoundrel." Sunday reached out a hand and coaxed his dark hair back behind his ear.

Half the room gasped.

Sunday didn't care.

That night in bed, Sunday wrote about her very long day, about her dress and the people at the ball. She wrote about her sisters and their escapades. She wrote that she had made a friend, and that she had danced every dance. But she did not mention the prince to Grumble, to what would be to Grumble when she saw him again. It pained her to not be able to speak of the happiness that brimmed to overflowing inside her, but she did not feel comfortable mentioning this man to her best friend. This man who was a man, and not a frog. This man who was not just a man, but a prince. A prince who was her father's sworn enemy.

A prince she was falling in love with.

The next day started so much like the one before it that it took Sunday a while to realize the previous night hadn't been a dream. She awoke to her mother yanking the book out from beneath her head and scolding her for letting the candle burn down. Sunday yawned and rose to get started on her chores...and then noticed the silver dress in the corner. She clasped her pillow to her breast and allowed herself two gluttonous minutes of dancing around the room before she sobered and took the dress downstairs for Friday to alter for the night's festivities.

Saturday "injured" herself in the Wood that day, and she limped around the house quite convincingly until Mama caved and told her she did not have to go to the ball. The hired carriage was a little less cramped that night, and Sunday thought Papa seemed happier to have one of his girls stay behind to keep him company. He still looked at Sunday wistfully as she mounted the carriage steps, and she wondered if it was her resemblance to Tuesday that made him sad, or if he could see through her skin to her traitorous heart.

Friday had done wonders retrimming Sunday's dress with gold, Wednesday's with blue, and hers and Mamas with pieces of silver from Sunday's the night before. But this night was different, and there were so many people at the palace that the Woodcutter women were instantly swept up in the crowd and separated from each other as soon as they alighted from the carriage. Sunday called out to her mother and sisters, but she could not hear them above the din of the voices that surrounded her. Her heart began to race again, and goosebumps rose up on her skin. She looked around frantically.

The two girls next to her turned...and snarled.

Sunday didn't see who landed the first punch, the one that connected with her stomach and made her double over as she struggled to regain her wind. She could not tell how many hands tore at her ribbons and ripped her dress to shreds, she only heard their shrieks like wild animals above the rending of fabric. Someone's pointed slipper connected with her ribs, and she knew that if she did not stand, she would surely be killed. Her cheek was scratched, and soot was rubbed into her hair and pushed into her mouth. Somehow she blindly made her way to a wall of the castle, found a door, and fell inside the kitchen to safety.

One scullery maid bolted the door, while another sat Sunday down by the fire and held a damp cloth to her wounds. Sunday begged a third not to tell the prince. Which she could only assume is exactly what the girl did once she passed out.

Words and small images came and went through Sunday's consciousness. She was lifted up into strong arms, and a fresh dress was ordered for her. She was changed and tidied and her wounds were tended to by women with soft hands who sounded like silk and smelled of lilacs. She was taken to a place where nightingales sang in the trees above and the sounds of a party could be heard floating in the distance on the cool night air.

Sunday awoke with her head on soft velvet, her hand covering a royal gold medal.

"They will only hate me more for making you miss your own ball," she said to the prince from his shoulder.

"The hellions should be grateful I did not call off the evening altogether. I have never seen such savagery."

"The female of the species..." Sunday chuckled, and her ribs suddenly regretted it.

"It is my fault for singling you out."

"It is my fault for wanting to be singled out," Sunday fought back, "and the curse of an interesting life. There are very good times and very bad times. Black and white. Things aren't usually nice shades of grey. Tonight was the price I paid for having such a wonderful time yesterday."

"Do not attempt to justify their actions," said the prince. "You deserve better. From all of us." He smoothed her hair with his hand, and she was too weary and too selfish to tell him to stop. "This will not happen again tomorrow."

Sunday lifted her head from the prince's shoulder and looked him in the eyes. "There can be no tomorrow, surely you realize that."

"There will be. I will send a carriage at sundown, and my guardsmen will accompany you and your family to the Entrance. You have my word; no harm will come to you."

But that's not it at all, she wanted to tell him. Don't you see how far I am beneath you? Don't you see that my family doesn't have enough money to afford three dresses for each of their daughters for a ball every night? Don't you remember that I'm a Woodcutter, and that your evil fairy godmother turned my brother into a dog and my father will never give me permission to...to...

She let the manic words winnow away to nothing. Her heart

was gone; she had betrayed her friend and her family, and whatever happened, happened.

"Thank you."

"And now," said the prince as he lifted her into his arms, "I will send you home to rest. I will go back to the party and tell your mother that you have fallen ill with fatigue as a result of the crowd."

He was good; that wasn't entirely a lie. "I can walk, you know."

He ignored Sunday's protests. "And then I will woo your mother and dance with your sisters all night until every other woman in the room is green with envy."

She swatted his shoulder. "Beast."

He sat her down gently in the carriage and kissed her hand.

"Good night, my Sunday."

"Good night, my prince."

The house was dark when Sunday arrived home, and she was grateful. She quietly and carefully climbed the stairs to her tower room and eased the new dress over her bruised body. She threw back the covers of her bed and saw her book, small and lonely on the pillow.

But Sunday could not bring herself to write the words.

She turned her face into the pillow and cried herself to sleep.

When Mama poked Sunday awake the next morning, she screamed.

"I'm sorry," she said quickly. "You startled me."

"You have more to be sorry for than that. You started quite the scandal, disappearing off with the prince last night."

"I was...ill."

"So ill you ruined your dress?" Mama scoffed. "Don't lie to me, Sunday. It isn't you." Sunday opened her mouth, but Mama held up a hand. "Don't tell me the truth either, because I don't want to lie to your father. Just tell me this. Are you in love with him?"

"Yes." All Sunday's torment filled up that one word and spilled over the sides.

"That's what I was afraid of."

And then the strangest thing happened.

Mama softened.

"Come with me, child."

Sunday followed her mother down the tower steps to her parents' room in the main house. Mama led her to the trunk at the end of her bed, a fixture for so long Sunday had forgotten it was there. She pulled off the quilts and pillows that were stacked on top of it, and the lid creaked as she pried open the long-neglected hinges.

Inside the trunk was a box, and inside the box was a dress of silver and gold, the most beautiful dress Sunday had ever seen.

"It was Tuesday's gift from Fairy Joy," Mama said after a prolonged and reverent silence, "for when she danced at her wedding." There was a hitch in her voice. "She never got to wear it." She looked up at me with damp eyes. "I think she would want you to have it."

The world around her clicked, and Sunday saw what was really going on, what Mama was really saying.

Seven for a secret never to be told.

Just as the things Sunday wrote came true, things Mama said came true. She had stopped having children after seven daughters. She had called Trix a member of the family and he was, and it never occurred to anyone to think differently. She had called Sunday ungrateful...and everyone knew how successfully *that* had developed. It was Mama who had said the shoes would never wear out, and in doing so she had cursed her own daughter to death. Mama who had said that one of her daughters would be engaged by the end of the week, and so cursed Sunday as well.

It wasn't Tuesday who wanted Sunday to have the dress; it was Mama.

Sunday hugged her mother tightly. "It's beautiful, Mama."

Seven Woodcutter put her awkward arms around her youngest daughter. "I love you, Sunday. No matter what happens."

For once, Mama didn't have to say it for Sunday to know it was true.

Mama, Wednesday, Friday and Sunday were all ready when the prince's carriage arrived at sunset.

This time, her father was not at the door to watch them leave.

When they arrived at the palace, there was no need for an escort, as guards lined the path from the stairs to the Grand Entrance. They walked through the doors that opened before them, and when they were announced, the assembly bowed as one.

Sunday had to restrain herself from running down the red-carpeted stairs to take the hand of her prince.

"Don't you think this is a bit much?" she whispered.

"No. You look beautiful."

"Thank you."

"Shall we dance?"

The music started up at once, as if the musicians had been waiting the whole time for Sunday's arrival. She could almost feel the collected relief as other dancers began to fill the floor. Sunday and her prince danced countless dances straight before stopping for a breath of fresh air on the prince's private balcony. He immediately sent his servant for wine and refreshment.

"I hated letting you go last night," he said as soon as they were alone. "The party wasn't the same without you."

"I missed you too." The truth hurt just as badly when spoken aloud. This was all too painful, and she had to put a stop to it. She wondered, after so long, if Grumble even remembered her, but she had betrayed her father long enough.

"Your Highness—"

"My friends call me Rumbold."

Sunday could not let herself sink deeper into the mire by addressing him so familiar.

"Sunday," he asked softly, "will you be my friend?"

He was killing her. "*Your Highness*, we can't be anything. This can't go on any longer. Surely you know who I am, who my family is."

"The past is past," he said. "Can't we put it behind us?"

How could he shrug off such a tragedy so lightly? He didn't know the impact her brother's fate had had on her family. He couldn't have. For all his princely life, locked up in his ivory tower, Sunday could see that he was blissfully unaware of the exact situation. She was determined to clear the air between them.

She held up a hand to his mouth. “Please, let me finish.” He said nothing, only began to kiss her fingers and she was forced to concentrate. “I am a *Woodcutter*,” she said, determined to make him understand. “Sunday *Woodcutter*.”

“And you're ungrateful,” he finished. “I already know that part.”

Sunday blinked, and all the familiar words finally hit home. The world spun around her, and for the second time that night it clicked – slammed – horribly into focus.

Grumble.

Rumbold.

The prince hadn't been off on holiday, he had been enchanted.

That last kiss had broken the spell.

The trading of the golden bauble for royal tokens; him picking her out of the crowd only seconds after her arrival at the ball on the first night.

He had been in love with her the whole time.

Prince Rumbold's eyes twinkled and he kissed her fingers again.

Oh, she was such a fool.

A dog's faraway howl at the moonlight snapped her out of her shock, and she turned and fled.

This time the hellion horde worked in her favor; they were all too eager to see her leave, and all too happy to mob the prince and slow his pursuit. Sunday heard her sisters' voices calling after her, but she did not stop for them. She did not stop for anyone, until she met Trix on the carriage way. He was sitting on the steps there, as if he had been waiting for her.

"Come," he told her. "I will run with you."

She didn't think to tell him it was no use, that the prince would no doubt have his horse saddled and overtake them, that he would release the hounds and they would nip at their heels until he arrived. She followed Trix through the fields and the scrub woods, until the baying and the hoofbeats were almost upon them.

They stopped beside a small pond.

"They will catch us," Sunday said to Trix.

"We will hide," said Trix.

"How?"

"You have to believe," he told her. "Just like when you write, or Mama speaks. If you believe we can hide, we will be hidden."

Sunday grabbed her brother's hands, closed her eyes, and believed with all her might. She believed so hard that when the prince slowed his horse by the pond, she believed he did not see a woman in a gold and silver dress and her wild brother, only a tree with gold and silver rosebuds on it and a rock beside it. She believed that he sat on the rock and buried his head in his hands, and that when his shoulders shook he was not laughing. She believed that he stood up, plucked a rose from the tree, and rode back off towards the palace. And when he was gone, she believed that Trix stood up and cracked his sore back, and that she ran beside him, half barefoot, all the way home and into her father's arms.

Sunday woke the next morning and put on her nicest gown, for though she had made peace with her family, she knew that she wouldn't be able to run from the prince.

Papa did not go out to the Wood that morning, and Mama limited her daughters' chores to tasks around the house. They would all be there for Sunday when Prince Rumbold came.

His carriage arrived shortly after breakfast.

The Woodcutters met him outside, under Trix's tree.

Prince Rumbold bowed to Papa. "Sir, I have come to heal the breach between our families."

Papa did not bow in return. "You have taken my son from me," he said. "You will not take my daughter as well."

"Forgive me, sir, but your son's refusal to return home had nothing to do with me."

"You killed him." Papa face turned red and hard. "Your murdering family cursed him and killed him."

Prince Rumbold did not back down. "The *wolf* killed him, sir. Not anyone from my family. When I returned his medallion to you, I hoped that the ill will would end there." He clasped his hands behind his back. "I see it did not."

"Now see here..." Papa's words were punctuated by spittle as his anger grew.

Mama laid a calm hand on Papa's breast and stepped toward the prince.

"Wolf?" The word barely had enough strength behind it to push its way from her reluctant mouth. "What wolf?"

"If you please, mum. I only know the story as I lived it, and even that can be tainted by the ever-changing memories of a young boy. Your son killed the dog my father gave me for my birthday, and for his penance, my fairy godmother cursed him to serve in the dog's place for a period of one year. In return, *his* fairy godmother placed a curse on *me*, that upon my eighteenth birthday I would live as an amphibian for the same period of time," he smiled at Sunday, "a period that was most happily shortened by a certain maiden and her kiss of true love."

"A year?" That certainly wasn't part of any of the stories and songs Sunday had ever heard. "Papa, is this true?"

"He was turned into a dog," said Papa, "and he never returned home."

"After a year, Jack returned to human form and was allowed to stay at the castle to recover. Knowing that I would one day share his fate, to some extent, I approached him. My desire for knowledge overrode my fear of him. He admired my youthful bravery, and we became friends."

"Lies!" shouted Papa. "Why should we believe any of this?"

"Because I know things about Jack that others could not know," said the prince, "things he would not have confided to anyone who was not a true friend. That medallion for instance."

Papa pulled the medallion from beneath his shirt almost unconsciously.

"Jack was born a sickly child, and it was thought that he would not survive his infancy. But on his nameday, his fairy godmother gifted him with that medallion, so that it might give him strength."

Papa's eyes were wide; his jaw clenched tightly.

"Surely that is something only a confidant would know. Certainly not someone who was your son's enemy."

Papa seemed eager to speak at that, but Mama's hand still remained firmly on his chest.

"A year," Mama encouraged Prince Rumbold to continue.

"Jack was released from my family's household fourteen years ago," said Prince Rumbold, "and he continued about his adventures and heroics, his flights of fancy and feats of unsurpassed bravery. His last valiant effort came about saving a young girl from a wolf...which he did. But not before the wolf claimed his prize. I myself sliced open the wolf's belly. The medallion was all that remained. And so I returned it to you, sir, explaining everything. You obviously received it."

Sunday imagined she looked much as her sisters did at the present moment – mouth agape and brows furrowed in confusion.

But none of them could compare to the sheer stillness that Seven Woodcutter had become, her silence almost tangible in the air. Mama blinked, and then turned eyes of fire upon Papa. Sunday tried to imagine what thoughts raced behind those eyes. Her own husband had lied to her, and kept that lie safe for over a decade simply to dwell in his own petty hatred. The medallion that had returned to them after so long had indeed marked Jack's death...but that mark was the punctuation at the end of a life, a life she had never known he had. The songs written after Jack's disappearance were true. Her son had lived. And she had been the worse betrayed.

"You will not marry my daughter." Papa's command did not carry the strength of his previous rantings.

Mama's hand dropped from Papa's chest. "Yes." The one word

dripped ice and cut like a razor. "Yes, he will. It has been said. The words have been spoken. And not even you can change that, Jack Woodcutter."

In Sunday's heart glimmered a spark of hope she had thought long dead.

Mama took her hand. "Sunday, do you love this man?"

Sunday loved him as a man and a frog and a prince; she loved him with all her heart as surely as she loved her own family.

"Yes, I do."

Mama placed Sunday's hand inside Rumbold's. "Then you have our blessing."

As if someone were moving his head, Papa nodded. Without another word, he turned and headed into the Wood. Mama led her daughters into the house. Prince Rumbold and Sunday found themselves alone in the yard. Trix rustled above them in his treehouse.

Sunday and her prince stared at each other for a very long time.

"I have something for you," he said finally.

"You do?"

He nodded. "You seemed to have misplaced a recurring theme." From behind his back he produced Sunday's silver and gold slipper from the night before. "I felt it was only proper to return it."

Sunday laughed, and with that laugh the birds sang and the sun shone and the flowers bloomed. Hope blossomed inside her, and she felt alive once again.

"I cannot promise you a happy ending," she admitted. A tendril of the magic beanstalk curled around her finger and a leaf opened up in her hand. "But I can promise you an interesting life."

"A man could not hope for a better future."

They smiled at each other.

"If I may be so bold, Miss Woodcutter…" he started.

"Please, call me Sunday."

"Sunday," he smiled again. "Do you think you could find it in your heart to kiss me?"

Sunday had wondered how long it would take before he got around to asking.

The Cursed Prince

The aggregate history of Rumbold,
Crown Prince of Arilland

Fate knows the destinies of soulmates; the gods whisper them in her ear and she keeps them close to her breast. But fey-bloods know the burning desire of all hopeless humans (and even some hapless fairies) to unlock Fate's diary, read all her intimate secrets, and carelessly meddle in the delicate matters of the heart. And so the Fairy Wells were created, and the Wells begat the Well-Wishers.

The recipe is simple enough for any school child to remember: toss gold into the well to wish for love, silver to keep it, and cold iron to dissolve it. Of course all of the stories involving that last one never work out the way the wisher means them to, and most often the outcome is not in the wisher's favor.

The children of Arilland learned all those stories at their mother's (or father's) knee, and took heed to always be wary of what they wished for. Fate might know a man's destiny, but how badly he screws up the path to get there is entirely up to him.

Rumbold did a better job of screwing up than Fate ever could.

She smelled like lavender. Or was it lilacs? Rumbold buried his nose deeper into the sleeve of his mother's gown as she told him the story of the Giant of Tinnyran for the hundred hundredth time. Violets? It was one of those flowers he knew, one of the light purple ones that dared defy winter and burst into spring every year against all odds and fell to pieces anytime he tried to touch it.

They're all the same, thought the young prince. *She just smells purple*.

He smiled into the sound of her voice as it echoed through her skin. It did not matter that she had told him a hundred hundred times about the giant and the boy who tricked him into giving him a ride on his shoulders. He could easily have heard it a hundred more. Every time she told the story it was new and exciting. Every time he was scared that the giant would squeeze the boy into paste or grind his bones and lick the boydust off his fingers. And every time the boy sat on the giant's shoulders and saw the whole world stretched out before him, Rumbold's eyes watered at the beauty of it too. But in that hundred hundred times, Rumbold never remembered a yellow-green dragon breathing the fire of the sun down upon them…

"Mother," he giggled. "That's not how it goes."

"If you know the story so well," Mother mock-scolded, "perhaps you should tell it to me instead."

"But I cannot," said Rumbold, "because...I have a very rare disease that makes me forget a story instantly after I hear it."

"Is that why you keep asking for the same story over and over?"

"I've heard it's an excellent story." His feigned sternness became giggles as she attacked him. She would not stop until he begged for mercy, and then she scooped him up into her springly purpleness and squeezed him tightly. Any tighter and Rumbold might turn to paste himself, or the two of them might be squeezed into the same skin, never to be separated.

Not that he would have minded. Laughter always filled the air around his mother. People smiled in her wake as she passed them in the halls, as if they had suddenly been overcome with joy and couldn't help themselves. She was the epitome of fun and innocence and life, and she was so very, very beautiful.

So very, very unlike his father.

He had asked her many times before what it was that had made her fall in love with the stern, unfeeling, heartless king. "Oh, my solemn son," she laughed, "where's your sense of adventure?" And because she had laughed when she answered him he smiled and knew that whatever the reason it was a good reason, for his mother could not have imagined the world any other way. If she was happy, Rumbold was content. Happiness was her gift.

All fey have gifts.

The king liked to surround himself with fairies and fey-bloods.

It was common knowledge that proximity to someone with fairy blood elongated one's lifespan, and while no one could remember exactly how old their handsome king was, they knew he had been around long enough to outlive one queen and marry another while still in his prime. Rumbold recalled the prevalence of dark-hair among the dignitaries at court, darker than his mother's long chestnut curls, but none of them with tresses as black as Velius...

"Am I fey?"

Soft fingers paused in their meandering trail across his furrowed brow and slid down his cheek. "My never-constant son. What makes you ask such a thing?"

"The boys at the training ground today said that Velius was fey."

"Velius. The duke's son."

Rumbold nodded. Velius was a duke's son, but nobody ever called him that.

"Well, they're right in any case," she answered. "It's too late an hour for me to go into, but yes. Your cousin has more wild fairy blood in him than anyone I've ever met." She looked away, and the lamplight turned her blue eyes golden. "Almost anyone," she added as an afterthought. "What does any of that have to do with you?"

"The other children say that I'm fey too, because I have dark hair."

Contagious as his mother's laugh usually was, it didn't make Rumbold feel instantly better. The enthusiastic kiss she placed on his forehead did. The pillow haloed her dark brown curls around her as she settled back down and took a deep breath. Rumbold knew that breath meant a story, so he closed his eyes and snuggled into her warm body again.

"Faerie is a land so large its size mirrors the human world—perhaps even surpasses it; no one knows for sure. Deep in the heart of Faerie lives the Fairy Queen. She is its only Queen, and has reigned over the land since the beginning of time. Her hair is as black as night, her skin as white as pearl, and her eyes are deep violet, as deep and rich as dragon's blood.

"She has no children because she cannot; in order to give life to another being of her own flesh, she would have to sacrifice so much of herself and her power that there would be nothing left. But it is said that those humans with the most fey blood in their hearts look very much like the Fairy Queen."

"And they have special powers?"

"Gifts. Some of them have gifts, yes."

Rumbold let her story wrap itself around him, painting him her shade of purple. What if he had dragon's blood in his veins? Could he do wonderful things? But Mother had not said the gifts were wonderful, only that they were beyond comprehension.

"But there are many fey-bloods inside and outside Faerie with skin as black as pitch or hair as white as snow, or both. There are some so good at what they do that you would never notice, and some so inept they can't make decent tea." Rumbold smiled at the thought of a fairy dropping a teakettle and having an army of salamanders scurry out of it and across the floor. "They come in all shapes and sizes, just like humans. And you, my dearest," she tapped him on the nose, "may have eyes and hair as brown as treestain, but you are as human as they come. Just like your father."

Rumbold wasn't sure how he felt about that. He didn't want to be "just" anything. Especially if it meant he had to be like his father.

Her graceful fingers ruffled his hair. "And before you ask, my curious one, yes. I do love your father. I love him because he is our king, and because without him there wouldn't be you."

"I know," sighed Rumbold. He always sighed when she left, and the leaving tone was in her voice.

"Good night, baby," she said, as she said every night, and kissed him on the cheek.

"But I am not a baby," Rumbold answered, as he always did now. "I am a grown boy and train with the palace guards."

"So true." She kissed him again heartily, this time on the opposite cheek. "Then I wish you pleasant dreams, your highness."

"But you are the queen" he said. "I am not higher than you."

"Certainly not taller," she chuckled and kissed him again. "I love you, my son. For you cannot argue that you are not my son."

"No, I cannot. Good night, Mother. I love you too."

He squeezed her hand in the hopes that she might change her mind, as he had every night since he could remember, as he would every night for the next hundred days. But she still left him, as she had and did and ever would, then and the hundred nights after, until she left his room for the very last time. That night was no different than any of the others, and he would not have had it any other way. But never again did he smile into the darkness after her, his hair a mess against the pillow, the lingering scent of purple in the air, and the pressure of her lips still faint on his cheeks.

He snuggled back into his mother's arms for warmth, not for himself, but for her. With every day she grew weaker and colder; his small body had become the source of heat for them both. Her arm was like marble cradled around his belly; he spread his palms against her skin and wished his strength into her flesh. He willed her breath to fall deep and even, for the heartbeat against his spine to come harder and faster, pushing the life back through her veins. Her once indigo eyes were now a dull blue, when she decided to open them at all. Her cheeks had faded from pink, to white, to a yellow-gray pallor. That color scared Rumbold.

The prince pulled tight into a ball. He imagined he was a human coal, burning with a fire so bright and hot that his mother would not—could not—bear to leave him. He cherished the pressure of her fingertips when she squeezed his knee, his arm, his fist every so often, felt the love and promises and memories as they danced lazily from her soft, faint voice through his hair. He held her hand up to the light that sliced across them from the slightly open door to the outer chambers. He tried to memorize the shape of that hand, the size of it against his own, wanting to burn the memory into his mind forever. Life was fleeting, his little ears had heard one of the chambermaids say, and the queen rushed toward its end so fast that no one could catch her, tell her to wait, or remind her of what she was leaving behind.

The flesh of her hand was translucent now, fading as she was, and it cast no shadow on his own. But Rumbold would not remember the sick shell the gods were slowly erasing from life's canvas; he would remember the stories and the laughter, the wavy hair and the merry eyes, the lilac and the lavender. He would remember this hand, beautiful and imperfect, and his mind's pencil would draw love, solid and substantial, along the curve of every nail and the wrinkle on every knuckle. She would leave him, as everyone left in time, but nothing could steal his memories.

"I ask you this a third time."

"And thricely I refuse."

Rumbold made himself as small as he could, slipping under the coverlet and sinking back into his mother with as little movement as possible. He did not want his father or godmother to see him there. They would take him away again and send him back to his own bright rooms with the colors that failed to disguise the chill in the walls and floor. The sun's rays that fell in the window held no joy; there was nothing there but the constant reminder of how he could not help his mother. Here, with her, he could pretend. He could be the hot coal, and the queen's soul might rub its hands together over his fire for one moment longer.

"But I—"

A silence interrupted the king, a rustle of fabric, and another silence that might have been the walls of the castle sighing, succumbing to the weight of the world. Quiet though it was it had not come from his mother; the queen's pulse still beat tentatively at his back.

"Your feelings are not unrequited," said Sorrow. "But blood will turn to gold, your wife will die. When the time comes again you will bind yourself once more to a fey woman, and she will not be me. Such is the way of things."

"And you will never walk beside me."

Sorrow barked the harsh laugh of a brazen crow refusing to be tempted by sparkling in the sand. "I will never walk in your shadow, my love. I will never be your tool, and I will never be your queen." The silence came again, stolen and quick. "But I will ever be beside you, for as long as we both shall live."

"So be it." His father did not sound happy. Rumbold had never heard anything in his father's voice besides duty.

"Tomorrow you will feast on foul and face a future fit to contain another lifetime of foolishness," said his godmother. "Tonight you must mourn."

Rumbold could hear their footsteps now as they approached, and the sliver of golden light that fell over them from the crack in the door grew wider. Rumbold huddled down even further and closed his eyes, refusing the light.

"Don't be afraid," Mother whispered in his ear, softer than sheets, softer than stone. Her hand fell away from his side and she settled back into the pile of feather pillows the chambermaids had brought for her comfort and left regardless. A bundle of down could never replace the healing properties of a little boy, no matter how heavily either was hidden in satin.

"I am still here, husband," she announced to the room with a strength Rumbold was surprised to hear her muster. "A situation I will be sure to remedy shortly." Her laugh was a wheeze blown over the lip of a bottle.

"I am sad to hear it." He wasn't, though.

Her heartbeat skipped; the strength she had found seemed to be outpacing her on the sands of time. "You will not let my son see me die." The sentence was careful and clear, with a beat between each word that brooked no misunderstanding. Rumbold began to shake at her declaration.

"Look for me in your dreams." She whispered this into his skin and punctuated it with a kiss on his forehead from lips as dry as summer leaves. "I will be waiting for you there." Rumbold willed his body to cease its shivering, but it would not. He wanted to be a rock, a coal, a young man, a powerful prince, and he was ashamed at his body's betrayal.

Those were the last commands of Madelyn, High Queen of Arilland. Rumbold was quickly ushered out of the room by his godmother. The queen reportedly died in the night, peacefully, and no one ever laid eyes on her again.

Rumbold did not eat for days. He did not speak for over a month. Not that anyone but Rollins noticed, the one man who needed no commands to carry out his duties. This further lessened the prince's desire to share his thoughts with random castle folk. His father, on the other hand, had to keep up appearances. A lavish banquet was held in the queen's honor. The king drank to excess, spoke at volumes that made Rumbold's head ache, and consumed in one sitting an entire roast goose.

When Rumbold woke in the wee hours of the night the puppy was gone. He missed the warm nose squirming under his arm like he missed his mother. Mother was soft and sweet and smelled of safety and love. She used to lie in bed beside him and tell him stories and stroke his cheeks with featherlight fingertips until he fell asleep.

It had been months since he had missed her so hard his cheeks were damp in the morning, but for a fleeting moment he felt the empty chill of waking up in a world without her. He shook his head, as if by chance the thought might wriggle its way out of his ears and flop on to the pillow. Thinking about Mother made him sad, and he didn't want to be sad.

He wanted his puppy.

The little brown and gold mutt had been generously promised to the young prince when he had stumbled across one of the palace bitches giving birth to her litter. The king had immediately denounced its existence. He frowned upon it and demanded that his son rid himself of the stinking, useless beast.

Out of spite, Rumbold treasured his puppy more than any other possession.

True, the pup was an unintelligent and sometimes stinky little creature, and caring for it took more work than Rumbold had ever done in his short life. It was so needy—always having to be fed or excused, forever wanting to play, constantly craving attention and love. Its deep, pleading eyes looked at Rumbold and saw father and brother, leader and playmate, provider and protector, master and ruler of the whole world. It refused to understand that Rumbold's heart had been broken too badly to love anything anymore, so

Rumbold cared for the puppy despite himself.

The neverending demands of the pup forced him to temporarily take up residence on the ground floor. With an eye to his safety, rooms had been prepared for him just off the wing of the Palace Guard. No matter the hour Rumbold was never alone when he took the pup out to the yard...to where the restless animal had no doubt disappeared.

Rumbold eased out of bed and tiptoed across the cold stones, not wanting to wake Rollins for a robe and slippers. The chamber door was open a puppy-sized crack. Rumbold widened it to boy-sized and slipped through.

He paused in the candlelit corridor, calming his galloping heart enough to listen for whispers in the shadows. Nothing. They had not followed him here. Not that it gave him much comfort; he was sure the whispers would return to haunt him at any moment. It was only a matter of time before they discovered this new place. He hurried along.

He wasn't familiar enough with the labyrinth of new corridors to know the way without Rollins. Of course, the puppy wouldn't have known either, which was just as well. His father said a good hunter must know his prey. Rumbold concentrated and tried to think like a mischievous puppy. The left end of the hallway led to quiet candles and more darkness. The right end of the hallway was much the same, but further down there was a richer, orangish sort of glow and the faint sounds of men's voices.

That way.

A few more twists and turns brought him to the Guards' Hall.

Rumbold peeked around the corner carefully, so as not to be discovered and sent back to bed.

His father's men sat around tables, eating and drinking and talking and laughing in deep, seemingly bottomless tones that Rumbold couldn't imagine himself possessing one day. Now and again scraps from the table would be nonchalantly tossed to the rushes, where the palace hounds would playfully fight over them.

The prince squinted into the light tossed about by the fire and wall sconces until he found his squat little prey, dancing in a forest of legs thick and thin, man's and dog's. Rumbold balled his small hands into fists, wondering how he would get his pup to heel without attracting the attention of the whole room. If his father discovered that he had left his chambers unnoticed as a result of the animal's behavior, he would certainly and immediately deprive Rumbold of the puppy...or worse.

He stifled a giggle as he watched the older dogs playfully tease the pup with scraps. He hoped they didn't feed him overmuch; on a previous occasion the pup's belly had become distended enough to hamper his ability to walk. Amusing as it was at the time, the prince did not find it amusing later, when the sick pup emptied his insides from both ends.

An older dog pulled at a scrap with the pup and then let the little one win, sending him tumbling back into the leg of one of the guards. Startled, the pup turned on instinct and nipped at the offending ankle. Like a cow bit by a fly Rumbold watched as the muscle of the leg twitched and the foot jerked, sending the weightless puppy sailing into the stones of the fireplace.

Rumbold was not worried. The pup had many times proven to be remarkably resilient. He would pop up, shake himself off, and jump at another scrap.

Any moment now.

One of the older dogs moved to the unmoving body and nudged it with his nose. Another dog let out a small whimper. A high-pitched, unbroken wail filled the room.

All eyes turned to Rumbold's hiding place.

He realized the wail was coming from him.

The candle flames dipped and trembled and there was a cold breeze at his back. Long, thin fingers tipped by ebony nails slid over his shoulder. "Shhh, dearling," the dark voice hissed. "Your godmother is here now."

Rumbold wished the screaming would stop, but he could not seem to shut his mouth. He wished he could move. He wished he could breathe. He wished that all the things he loved would stop leaving him.

The icy fingers squeezed in a comforting gesture, but Rumbold did not want comfort. He wanted vengeance. His stiff arm rose as if lifted by godstring, his finger pointing at the tall, blond guard who rubbed his ankle absentmindedly.

The fingers squeezed again and the fire in the fireplace extinguished itself, filling the whole room with a similar chill.

The guard's red-bearded companion turned to him. "Jack, what have you done?"

It happened each afternoon like clockwork, but Rumbold didn't indulge himself by taking advantage of every opportunity. It would be dangerous for his own habits to become as predictable as Master Lucian's. Nor did the prince want his current lackadaisical Studies Master to be replaced by a tutor made of sterner stuff. So when the clock in the outer chamber rang two bells and Master Lucian settled back in his comfortable chair to sleep off his noon meal, Rumbold did not always escape.

When he did, he made egress by way of the portrait hall, where generations of kings and queens hung immortalized by the hands of the finest artisans of their time. Each monarch had left to this land great legacies of children and laws. Of battles won and lost. Of lands conquered, allies garnered, and foes slain. The years had made them memories, lines in sonnets and stanzas in songs, yet here they remained in perfect splendor for all time.

Rumbold tried to see some part of himself in each of the men and women before him. Had they preferred peas or potatoes? Would he grow into that stern expression or those wise eyes? Would he be pictured inside this castle, sitting by a fire, surrounded by items of peaceful benevolence? Or would he be bloody-armored on the battlefield, standing triumphant amidst the slain bodies of his enemies? Would he have champions so loyal to him that they would present him with rings of power and magic swords? Would he go mad and drink wine out of his shoes? When would his hair turn silver?

Sometimes Rumbold would forget his escape altogether and remain in the portrait hall, transfixed on some new minutia that had gone previously unnoticed: a dog at the foot of a chair, a dragon in flight outside a window, the lion's mane on a coat of arms.

He spent countless hours in front of the first queen. Not the first queen to have ruled Arilland—though at times he found her equally as fascinating—but his father's first wife, the woman who had preceded his mother. The whisper of a white gown draped over her willowy figure, and long silver hair spilled down over her shoulders. Her eyes were black, hollow, and…*incomplete* was the only word he could think to describe them, missing the robust confidence and substance of the queens before her. So much light surrounded her that she cast no shadow, but none of that brightness came from inside her. Each time he saw the queen's portrait Rumbold thought her thinner and frailer, more sad and more afraid, as if her body were fading from the painting little by little and might one day disappear forever.

The first queen's portrait never changed, but his father's did. And eventually, reluctantly, Rumbold would find himself there.

He never saw himself in the king, because he refused to look. It was hard to tell when it had been painted; his father appeared as a young man of indeterminate age. The king pictured did not look much older than his middling teen son, but neither did the portrait look much younger than the king did today.

The Portrait King stood alone in a grove, proud hands on his hips, proud chest outthrust. A wild wind mussed his crownless hair and ruffled his heavy cloak. His expression was one of arrogant selfishness and entitlement, a face that said he knew just what the world owed him, and he would take pleasure in exacting his due.

The attitude disgusted Rumbold and would have turned him away every time had it not been for the dynamic world that surrounded the Portrait King. The trees around him shifted with the seasons. Buds gave way to leaves that turned russet and fell to the ground over the course of the year. Birds nested, fed their young, and flew off to warmer climes. Flowers bloomed. Animals burrowed. Rain and snow fell, or had just fallen; the Portrait King never seemed affected by inclement weather.

And always, without fail, Rumbold's fairy godmother was there.

She never accompanied the king physically, but her presence kept a watchful eye on him from somewhere inside the frame. The suggestion of the curve of her body in the trunk of a tree; the image of her face formed by the leaves. An eye in the rain, or fingers on the wind. Rumbold would find himself torn between the challenge to seek her out each time and the fear that she would somehow find a way to escape the painting and haunt him the same way she haunted his father. But her eye never turned to Rumbold—it was ever fixed on the bold, immortal Portrait King. As Rumbold grew older he realized how beautiful his godmother was, a glamour enhanced by her terrible power, a power that had earned her a prestigious position in his father's court.

Long ago, in the annals penned by scholars in the age of the monarchs at the far end of the portrait hall, a disastrous curse had almost ended the royal line, and a valuable lesson was learned regarding the importance of certain fairies of significance. There were no "good" or "bad" fairies, but there were certainly those whose blood ran with a purer strain of the Wild Magic, who did not suffer fools and whose character tended towards impatience. These fairies had an affinity for mischief and an alliance with the chaotic monsters of the night. No one wanted to welcome such unpredictability, but trying to keep these fairies away inevitably brought upon the hosts a devastating retribution.

Early on, one particularly unlucky noble family decided to anticipate this disaster by inviting to their fete every fairy who had ever been suspected of doing anything malicious or vengeful. Unfortunately, the only thing fairies hate worse than having their powers insulted by humans is having their powers insulted by other fairies. The side effect of the fairies' resulting one-upmanship physically removed that kingdom completely from the face of existence.

Rumbold had searched his father's library for more on this subject, but as no traveler has ever returned from this kingdom, no one was ever able to confirm or deny the validity of the claim.

And so it became standard practice to formally invite one singular "bad" fairy to important events of state. In time, the title became one of fear and respect. By rolling out the red carpet for the most threatening creature shy of the Faerie Queen herself, a royal family might avert all future disaster.

Might.

By making Sorrow his personal advisor, Rumbold's father had secured her protections for as long as he reigned. By selecting her as the future king's godmother, he had effectively bound Sorrow for a lifetime. The castle would be safe as long as Rumbold lived, and with one of the most powerful fairies in the Land by his side, Rumbold's safety was assured.

But binding only meant obligation, not willingness. Safety did not mean love.

And vice versa.

He held the knife to his godmother's throat and realized he needed to leave this place. She stood still as a doe with a scent on the wind, her powdery-white skin reflecting in the bright blade. It was one thing to slip past an animal's defenses, but making the kill was another entirely. The former was merely a matter of intelligence. The latter was one of heart.

It took a certain kind of man to murder: a man who could slide off his conscience as he slid off his horse, a man who knew the right place, the right speed, the right pressure required, a man who could get the job done and move on. As ready as Rumbold might have been to take his own life, he knew he was not ready to take the life of another human—he squinted at Sorrow—or another almost-human. Sorrow had not so much as flinched when he had approached her. Those violet eyes knew his measure. It only served to fuel his anger.

He replaced the knife in its sheath, but did not back away. "I hate this waiting, waiting, *waiting*. I'm ready to get on with the rest of my life!"

"I know," was all she said.

He growled in frustration at the cherubs in the ceiling, as useless to him as anyone else. He was a prisoner in this castle, in his own body, until such time as Jack's godmother's countercurse came to fruition. It would have run its natural course on Rumbold's eighteenth birthday, but lo, his arrogant godmother had to test her skills and attempt the impossible. Thusly Sorrow had extended his sentence indefinitely. The prince's eighteenth natal day had come and gone and Rumbold had remained human. The people of Arilland had breathed a collective sigh of relief. Everyone, that is, save Rumbold. The curse hung low over his head like a dark cloud.

"I have to leave," he said.

"Go," said Sorrow. "But return on your birthday, so we will know when the curse comes to pass."

No apologies. No hope for the future. Her remarks should not have surprised him. His life had never been his own; as prince, he was the sole property of Arilland. No one truly cared what happened to him, as long as he remained hale and sound of mind, so that they all could go about their lives unbothered and unburdened. He was a face under a crown, a bum on a throne, a voice of reason only when there was none else to be had. He could be called a son or a man, but in truth he felt like neither. No one loved him for who he was; they loved him for *what* he was. And so long as that *what* disrupted everyone's lives as little as possible, it was allowed to exist.

Exist, yes, but no one said he had to stay. There was no sense in staying.

He remembered the reflection of Sorrow's pulse in his blade. His cold fairy godmother had a heart, but it only beat for itself.

Everyone in this palace was similarly selfish, it seemed. Only Rumbold's heart never beat on its own behalf. It beat for his father, for his subjects, for the good of the kingdom. Once upon a time, it had even beat for his mother.

No wonder he valued his life so little. He needed to stop living it for everyone else.

"Destiny knows your ending," Sorrow said to his back. "But you choose the path you take to get there."

"So I shall," he muttered. And so he did. That night he dressed in houseboy rags and stole a horse. He rode all day and night headlong to the coast and booked passage on the first ship out of the harbor. Leaving was far easier than he had imagined.

Becoming someone else was decadent.

Rumbold enjoyed the freedom of the open sea, the simple life on a ship, the possibilities of an entire as-yet-undiscovered world laid out before him. He enjoyed the salt mist and the clear, star-filled nights. He enjoyed the strange ports of call with their foreign smells that permeated the air and the food and the people. He enjoyed both the still and the storms. He even enjoyed the pirates.

The ship that bore him was easily taken and quickly plundered, and Rumbold attempted to prove his worth to the crew with a slim rapier that was more decorative than useful. His skills with said rapier could be similarly described; he discovered the hard way that pirates fought dirty. They did not fight by rules; they fought to win. The prince was quickly taken down by the pirate's first mate. He was named "Trouble" and marked as such. But they let him live. Moreover, they let him stay.

His real education began on board that tiny clipper ship, as far away from a dusty library and a hall of portraits as he could ever be. Rumbold learned the value of a hard day's work. He learned discipline and loyalty and camaraderie. He learned how to cheat at cards, how to lie both to women and with them, and how to steal a man's most treasured possession from right under his nose. Or behind his back. Or off his arm. Or out of his left breast coat pocket. He learned how to laugh, and how to make someone else do so in turn. He learned how far he could swim before his muscles cramped. He learned how many lashes he could withstand before his tears betrayed him. He learned how long a man could remain conscious in icy water, or without air. He learned the songs of the sea: the whales, the waves, the seals, and the sirens. He learned to guide himself by the stars so that he would never be lost, no matter how adrift he felt inside his soul. He learned how to sharpen both his knives and his wits. He learned how to be smart. He learned how to be selfish. There, on that ship, Rumbold learned to live.

It was also where he learned that he could not die.

Such knowledge would have frightened most men, but Rumbold had mastered his fear a decade ago at the bedside of one of the world's great heroes. And so he began taking risks: leading the charge onto captured ships, walking the rigging unharnessed, going after men fallen overboard without aid or warning. The more frequently he shamed Fate, the less necessary each act became until he was putting himself in danger simply for the sake of it. In his arrogance he missed the covert signal that the skipper had given to alert the guard.

He was apprehended in a tavern on the coast of Kassora and returned to the castle in Arilland on the eve of his nineteenth birthday. Just as before, that day that passed without incident or transformation. It was a day that meant everything to the kingdom and nothing to the young man they celebrated.

Next year, Rumbold decided, there would be no celebration. No one celebrated someone they despised. His future feats would be reckless enough to make Jack Woodcutter wince. He would become *infamous*. Oh, yes. They'd be telling his stories for years.

He had to find Sunday. Somehow, he would make her see the insanity of these familial politics. His true love was too intelligent to let an incredible life slip away because of one emotional decision made by a very small boy so long ago. It was all just a horrible accident, surely she could see that.

But she loved her family too much to toss the matter aside lightly.

Human once more, Rumbold abandoned the shattered remnants of the bucket and the moss-covered rocks and the ruins of the well that had been his shelter for so many months.

Despite the whipping of the wind and the rumble of the sky, he vowed to see this through to the end...whatever it took.

He remembered the encounter with Sunday's mother in the backyard that first afternoon. Fresh out of the transformation and clothed in naught but mud and scrapes, he had almost revealed a bit more to his true love at that point than either of them was ready for.

He could have told her that first night at the ball, revealed that he was her frog in prince's clothing. Rumbold played through a sample scene and dismissed it out of hand. She wouldn't have believed him, pure and simple. She wouldn't have wanted to believe. Her family hated his, plain and simple. Sunday Woodcutter would have turned and walked right back out of his life without so much as a fare-thee-well, the heels of her shoes leaving bloody footprints where they had crushed his stolen heart.

No, that wasn't true. She wouldn't have done that.

He would tell her things, things that only he knew, that only they spoke of, and she would have put her arms around him and hugged him tightly and maybe even cried a little and nothing, not even his father, would have been brighter than that moment.

But that moment had passed.

All the words he had were gone; there was nothing left in him to tell her that her good wishes were meaningless. He had already married Sunday a thousand times in his mind; nothing in the world had to change for Seven Woodcutter's prophecy to come true. There was no going back now, no rewriting the past. As truly as he loved her, he couldn't make her want him back.

"I wore Jack's medallion once, for a time."

Rumbold could still feel the ghost of its weight, hung from an imaginary silken cord.

"Did you know that? Do you know what such an object does to a healthy boy who does not need enhancements? It let me see beyond myself, realize my own potential, know the strength I would have if I became the best man I could possibly be. I made a great warrior and a good king, and every dream I had came true. But when I took it off I was just a boy again, the son of a cruel father and a dead mother in a life fraught with disappointment, the victim of a curse yet to come to fruition. I tried to be that good man. I tried until my future was pulled so far out of reach that my soul curdled and fell into despair. I damned that medallion and damned myself for ever having put it on.

"Jack was released from my family's household fourteen years ago," said Rumbold. "Uncursed, hale, whole, and fully human. He continued about his adventures and heroics, his flights of fancy and feats of unsurpassed bravery—all the adventures they sang about and more. His last valiant effort came about saving a young girl in the north from a wolf...which he did, but not before the wolf claimed his prize. I myself sliced open the wolf's belly."

He eyed the gold on Jack's father's chest. If Rumbold had the chance to wear the medallion again, what would it think of him now?

"The beast was empty. Jack was gone. That medallion was all that remained. And so I had it returned to you, sir, with a missive explaining everything. You obviously received it."

Jack Woodcutter Senior had lied to his wife. He had lied to them all and kept that lie safe for over a decade simply to dwell in his own petty hatred. The medallion that had been returned to his beloved's father marked the punctuation at the end of a life his Woodcutter siblings had never known he had. Whatever the rest of his story might have been, Jack Junior's tale had not ended in Arilland.

Seven Woodcutter's eldest son had lived.

Rumbold's heart went out to Sunday's mother. His own father was an evil, arrogant bastard, but he had never pretended to be otherwise.

"You will not marry my daughter." Woodcutter was adamant, but his command no longer carried the strength of his previous rantings.

Seven's hand dropped from her husband's chest. "Yes." The one word dripped ice and cut like a razor. "Yes, he will. It has been said. I have spoken the words. Not even you can change that, Jack Woodcutter."

A weathered hand reached out to him. Rumbold looked up into the steel gray eyes of his true love's mother. "Thank you," she said.

Rumbold nodded in acknowledgement and added no further explanations; he had done enough damage this night. Seven began to pull away until she noticed the tiny silver and gold shoe he held far too tightly in his hand. "Shall I take that back to her?"

He couldn't bring himself to release this last shred of Sunday. Not yet. Moreover, he didn't want to. "I'd like to return it myself," he whispered. "If you don't mind."

WARNING: SPOILERS AHEAD

Beyond this page lies the original Chapter 20 of the novel *Dearest*.

If you have not yet read *Dearest*, I strongly suggest that you do not read past this point. Because I love you and do not want you to ruin the story for yourself.

xox

~Alethea

Messenger

Dearest, Chapter 20

The messenger arrived the night before, though he did not make an appearance until daybreak. Conrad had no notice of the man's arrival, but for the sixth sense that all messengers have when someone else turns up bearing important information.

Instead of making his way to the palace, the man ran straight to the Guards' Hall. Conrad had watched his progress from the windows of the palace before running outside and tracing his footsteps like a whisper. Crouched in the hedges outside Duke Velius's chambers, he stayed just beyond the square of lamplight cast from the open window. He heard the messenger crash through Velius's door, presumably collapsing on the floor there.

"Erik!" the duke yelled at the man. "Erik!"

There was no answer. More guards arrived at the bedchamber door.

"He's exhausted," said the duke. "See if you can rouse him enough to for a hot bath, and then get him into bed. Have food waiting when he wakes."

There were grunting sounds as the guards complied with the order. Conrad nestled deeper into the bushes as the duke approached the window.

"Gods help him," Velius said to the starry sky. "Gods help us all. Eh, little bird?"

It was then that Conrad realized the duke was addressing *him*. He stepped out of the bushes as if it had been his intention to announce himself all along. "Yes, Your Grace."

"You are a wise and talented young man," said the duke's dark silhouette. "You will go far in this life, father than you have ever journeyed before."

"Thank you, Your Grace."

"I would recommend discretion at this time. I will not order you as a duke; I ask only as a man. A friend. A fellow soldier who cares for the princess you serve almost as much as you."

Conrad removed his hat and gave a small bow. He had witnessed Velius in action, seen him fight, knew a little of what great and terrible powers he could wield. "What is it you would have of me, Your Grace?"

"This has been an evening full of joy," said the duke. "I suspect the news my friend brings will unsettle us all once again."

Conrad suddenly remembered where he had seen the

messenger man before: upon his arrival at the palace in Arilland, dragging the body of a dead angel wrapped in a voluminous patchwork skirt—the angel he had come to know as Friday Woodcutter, the aforementioned princess who had taken him as her squire. The man had been bigger then, not stooped with fatigue, and his hair had been bright copper, not lank and dark with dirt.

Conrad wondered if King Rumbold appreciated the undying loyalty of those who served at his side. Tireless men like this guard, delivering his message at whatever cost. Wise men like Duke Velius, whose council took both the well being of his king and his country into consideration. Conrad had met a great many kings on his travels, and few could boast of such friendships.

"Wake your mistress after dawn," said the duke. "That should be plenty of time. I'll summon the rest of the family."

"As you wish, Your Grace." Conrad bowed again and sped off into the night.

At daybreak, Conrad returned from the kitchens with a warm pot of tea and some sweet rolls for Friday. He slid the tray onto the table and woke the princess as gently as he could, letting her know that she was wanted in the Great Hall. Then he slipped out the door and waited for her to ready herself.

Her talents undoubtedly sensed the anticipation in the air, because she was dressed in a flash.

"Should we fetch Tristan?" Friday asked as they made their way to the Hall.

"His presence was not requested," Conrad said formally.

Friday obviously caught his tone. "Goodness. Do you know what this is about?"

"No," Conrad said in earnest, for he did not. He only knew that the guard had arrived, not what message he bore, but he mentioned neither of those things to Friday. Conrad had learned the hard way the folly of delivering similar tidbits of vital information out of context.

As they entered the Grand Hall they saw the guard before them, cleaned and dressed and looking far less dire than he had upon his arrival. Friday ran to the man and embraced him. She, too, called him "Erik," as if he were simply another one of her brothers, but Conrad knew otherwise.

Erik swept the princess up into an enormous bear hug that made Friday giggle like a schoolgirl. The guard smiled at her laughter, but his worry lines remained. He set Friday down and politely greeted the rest of the Woodcutter family as they assembled before delivering his message.

Conrad noticed Erik's jaw tense slightly as Friday's ethereally beautiful eldest sister glided into the room. Neither the guard's body language nor his aura seemed threatening in any way, so Conrad maintained his post at a respective distance. When Princess Monday's eyes lit on the guard, however, his worry was accompanied by an immense sadness.

Duke Velius had been right. Whatever message Erik had come to deliver, it was not good. "I came from Rose Abbey as fast I could," he said without preamble.

"You just arrived?" the king eyed his guard's livery with suspicion.

"It was late in the night," Erik said humbly.

"And you waited until now?" Rumbold clicked his tongue. "I'm surprised, Erik. You're usually quite the gossipmonger. I expect better from you."

The guard did not rise to the king's jest, and the anxiety already building in the room became stifling. Immediately, the duke stepped forward. "Blame me," said Velius. "It was I who gave the order for Erik to wait."

King Rumbold sighed dramatically. "From you, Velius, I expect nothing but chaos." The king kept his jovial tone, but his wife and the rest of the Woodcutters remained tenuously silent.

"Last night was a time of reunion and happiness," said the duke. "I could not in good conscious ruin that for my king, my queen, or anyone else in Arilland." Velius looked to Friday specifically, who nodded. Her aura was still bright and aflame with love.

"Thank you for your consideration, Velius," Queen Sunday said in earnest.

"Besides, Erik stunk to high heaven. It was not a pretty sight. Or smell."

A few chuckles erupted in the room, including Erik's.

"Thank you for *that*," said the king.

"Can please I finish my story now?" Erik asked impatiently.

Both the king and the duke motioned for the guard to continue.

Erik addressed Queen Sunday. "Your Aunt Tesera is not dead;

she has fallen prey to a sleeping sickness." He paused, clenching his jaw before he spoke again. "I'm sorry, but your mother has also been struck by this affliction."

"Is it contagious?" The young Queen Sunday's voice bordered on hysteria.

"Is Saturday safe?" asked Friday.

"When is Saturday ever safe," said her brother Peter. "Is it a plague?"

"Only if the plague's name is Sorrow," said Erik. "The suspicion is that she's attacking all her sisters in order to steal their power."

"Can she do that?" asked Friday.

"If it's possible," said the duke, "Sorrow will find a way. And none of us will like the outcome."

"How was Aunt Rose when you left her?" Princess Monday delivered her question from her perch on the edge of an overstuffed chair. In her voluminous white gown, she looked pretty as a portrait.

"Determined," said Erik. "She will do everything in her power to protect her sisters while they are under her care. She believes the Abbey is the best place to mount a defense as any. Sorrow will have less power outside of Faerie."

Conrad had never before heard of this fey Sorrow, but he was predisposed not to like her.

"What of my other daughters?" asked Mr. Woodcutter.

"Thursday's ship had to leave without her when the ocean vanished, so she made her way westward, to the sea. Saturday and Peregrine traveled east to Faerie, to find Trix."

"Peregrine?" King Rumbold asked suspiciously.

"Saturday's *boyfriend*." Erik broke into a stupid grin completely inappropriate to the situation.

"You're kidding." Queen Sunday was clearly incredulous.

"Afraid not, Your Shortness. They're quite the pair. He's a prince from some godforsaken township in the frozen country and has a golden-eyed chimera for a pet. They've been under a spell all this time, and Saturday rescued them."

Golden eyes, thought Conrad. *Interesting*.

"That sounds like our Saturday," said Friday.

"You have no idea," said Erik. "She wears pants, he wears skirts, and the two of them can swing a sword as well as any of our guards here."

"I take it our girl finally got around to practicing," said Velius.

"Not much else to do while trapped in the White Mountains, I suppose. Between them they vanquished a witch and woke the Dragon of the North."

"They did *what*?" yelled Velius.

"Right," said Erik. "I hadn't mentioned the dragon yet, had I?"

The guard didn't have time to explain. There was a commotion at the door, and one of the two men stationed there poked his head in.

"What is it, Sir Griffin?" King Rumbold asked.

"Forgive me, sire, but there are three young people here to see you, and they will not be turned away."

"Send them in."

Conrad expected John, Wendy and Michael to come through

the doors. Three slender, towheaded children entered instead. The eldest was a girl of about sixteen. The boy looked a few years her junior. The youngest was small enough to be only five or six. Their clothes were simple, but their elegance did not go unnoticed by Conrad. The children bowed politely before the king and queen.

"We are Shear, Dart, and Pearl," said the eldest girl, presumably Shear. "We bring you both good tidings and bad."

"Let's have the good first, if you please," Queen Sunday requested.

"The esteemed seamstress Yarlitza Mitella is alive and well," said Shear.

An uncharacteristic whoop of excitement erupted from Friday at the news. "My dear mentor! How wonderful! She is safe?"

"As safe as houses," said the boy, Dart. "She broke her leg in the flood, but she still made it back home to us."

"She is our godmother," said Shear. "She swore to care for us if our mother ever fell ill. Unfortunately, that day has come to pass."

"Who is your mother?" asked the king. "From whence do you hail?"

"That's the bad news," said Dart. "Our mother's name is Teresa."

Conrad thought he had misheard the name. Hadn't the Woodcutter siblings already been notified of this aunt's illness? But the queen and her sisters all gasped at once. Conrad recalled Erik's announcement and realized that the name Shear spoken had been "Teresa," not "Tesera."

"Aunt Three," breathed Prince Peter, confirming Conrad's

supposition.

"The third Mouton sister struck down," said Mr. Woodcutter. "A sleeping sickness, no doubt?"

"Yes, sir," said Dart.

"This is ridiculous," said Mr. Woodcutter. "Sorrow must be stopped!"

Friday's father, already a bit of a giant, seemed to grow even larger in his fury. Friday stepped forward and took the hand of Pearl, the smallest girl, to keep her from being scared. Velius laid a hand on Mr. Woodcutter's shoulder and the large man calmed a bit, but his cheeks remained flushed and his eyes stayed wild.

"We will do what we can," said King Rumbold. "In the meantime, welcome, cousins. Please allow me to introduce you to your family."

"Thank you," said Shear.

"First, though," Dart said excitedly, "did I hear something about dragons?"

Once again, the room filled with laughter.

Conrad had told Friday that as soon as the atmosphere in Arilland stopped being strange and wonderful, he would return to the road. Omi had told Conrad that his journey would end when he found the place where his heart waited for him. He knew, deep down, that his soul had yet to find its true destination, but for now, he planned to stay right where he was.

ACKNOWLEDGEMENTS

For John Skipp, who invited me into an anthology called *Demons* and inadvertently gave me the rug that pulled "The Unicorn Hunter" together.

For Doug Warrick and Kyle S. Johnson, who invited me to write a story based on a Nick Cave song...and to my sister, Soteria, for choosing the perfect song for me.

For Brandi Hamrick, who flipped through the tiny notebook I keep in my car and asked, "What's a 'Vampire Mermaid'?"

For Jason Sizemore and Lynne M. Thomas at Apex, who were not afraid to publish a Romantic Young Adult Serial Killer Fairy Tale Retelling in a world when everyone else was.

For Eric James Stone—again and always—for unwittingly challenging me to include every single nursery rhyme and fairy tale I knew into a story, thus creating a Whole New World my brain would be happy living in forever.

And for Margo Mann Appenzeller, Casey Cothran, and Chris McCormick—because the geography of my world all started with the map we drew in high school. Arilland literally would not exist without all of us.

My hope is that Aria and Llandyr may yet still exist someday beyond these pages.

Continue on to read an excerpt from

TRIXTER

The Boy Who Talks to Animals

One more step. Two. Three. Three more steps. It was going to take him days to cross this meadow. Years. A lifetime. He deserved it, too, every moment of crippling agony, every scrape, every tear. Family didn't do this to each other. And yet...

Three days ago, he never would have put a sleeping spell on the stew and poisoned his sister, his brother, the man and woman who had raised him from a babe and never treated him like anything but their own. Three days ago, it never would have crossed his mind to do such a selfish and horrible thing. But three days ago his birthmother hadn't appeared in his dreams and called for him.

Earth breaks; fire breathes; waters bless. Fly to me, my son.

Trix knew what dreams looked like, the real dreams, the ones he was meant to pay attention to. They had more in them than the nothing-dreams of restless nights: more color, more feel, more sound, more taste, more cohesiveness, more details, more memory than memory. Real dreams did not fade upon waking but instead became more vivid, replaying themselves over and over in the mind's eye until the brain teetered on madness with the vision. Real dreams came from the gods. The gods knew how to make a point.

The gods also knew how to abandon someone in their time of need.

Trix would never have been able to convey the urgency of those dreams. The journey to Rose Abbey was one he needed to make immediately and alone. There was also a very good chance that the spell he'd put on the stew wouldn't work. It's not as if he had tried such a thing before—

PAIN.

Oh, the spell had definitely worked. Perhaps a little too well. Shame, too, because that stew had smelled delicious—one of his better accidental concoctions.

"It would have been nice to leave on a full stomach," he said, before recalling that no one was around to hear him.

Between the Woodcutter family and his animal friends, Trix was never alone in the world. And yet tonight there did not seem to be a soul within sight. Trix heard barely a cricket chirp above his ragged breathing. The twilight he escaped into offered a rare solitude. It was at the same time peaceful and concerning.

A silent Wood, in the main, usually meant trouble.

Trix stumbled again, forced himself back to standing and stayed there for a moment, listening. The wind had picked up.

Trix glanced over his shoulder—he could still make out the very top of the Woodcutter home just above the whipping, writhing grasses of the meadow. Dark clouds gathered in the west, swallowing the sun, but not before something in the tower window caught the fading light and flashed it back at him, like a lighthouse beacon on a foreign shore.

Like a warning.

The world fell completely silent then, as if Trix had stopped his ears with beeswax. The leaves were silent, his breath was silent, his heartbeat was silent. Even the wind was silent.

A moment later, the silence transformed into ceaseless thunder: first a low grumble, and then a growl as the earth bucked and reared, furious and alive.

The ground fell away before him. Trix came down hard on his knees. The meadow rolled beneath his feet, bending and waving like a sea of tall grass...on a sea of tall grass. He was caught up in the fray, helpless to regain his footing, so he tried to ride the earth as it slid and slipped beneath him.

He failed spectacularly.

ABOUT THE AUTHOR

New York Times bestselling author Alethea Kontis is a princess, a fairy godmother, and a geek. She's known for screwing up the alphabet, scolding vampire hunters, and ranting about fairy tales on YouTube.

Her published works include: *The Wonderland Alphabet* (with Janet K. Lee), *Diary of a Mad Scientist Garden Gnome* (with Janet K. Lee), the AlphaOops series (with Bob Kolar), the Woodcutter Sisters fairy tale series, and *The Dark-Hunter Companion* (with Sherrilyn Kenyon). Her short fiction, essays, and poetry have appeared in a myriad of anthologies and magazines.

Her YA fairy tale novel, *Enchanted*, won the Gelett Burgess Children's Book Award in 2012 and the Garden State Teen Book Award i 2015. *Enchanted* was nominated for the Audie Award in 2013, and was selected for World Book Night in 2014. Both *Enchanted* and its sequel, *Hero*, were nominated for the Andre Norton Award.

Born in Burlington, Vermont, Alethea currently lives and writes in Florida, on the Space Coast. She makes the best baklava you've ever tasted and sleeps with a teddy bear named Charlie. Connect with Princess Alethea online at: www.aletheakontis.com

CPSIA information can be obtained
at www.ICGtesting.com
Printed in the USA
LVOW07s0337030517
532999LV00003BA/800/P

9 781942 541059